*A
Harlequin
Romance*

OTHER
Harlequin Romances
by MARY BURCHELL

Many of these titles are available at your local bookseller, or through the Harlequin Reader Service.

For a free catalogue listing all available Harlequin Romances, send your name and address to:

HARLEQUIN READER SERVICE,
M.P.O. Box 707, Niagara Falls, N.Y. 14302
Canadian address: Stratford, Ontario, Canada.

or use coupon at back of book.

THE
BRAVE IN HEART

by

MARY BURCHELL

HARLEQUIN BOOKS   TORONTO
WINNIPEG

Original hard cover edition published
by Mills & Boon Limited.

This edition © Mary Burchell 1975

SBN 373-01871-1

Harlequin edition published April 1975

Printed in Canada

1871

CHAPTER ONE

"IT'S FUNNY," thought Jessica, "how aristocratically reproachful a dead salmon can look. Cod only achieves a huffy, middle-class stare, and herring are definitely cheerful and proletariat. But this salmon" — and she tried to look it firmly in the eye — "makes me feel dreadfully inadequate and low bred."

·To look a dead salmon in the eye and at the same time maintain one's balance on a bicycle, however, is not easy, even if the salmon is rearing its head out of the basket on one's handle-bars. And, after a moment, Jessica abandoned the attempt, and gave all her attention to pedalling as far as possible up the long hill home before she should be forced to dismount and push.

Past the three elms, clustered in a group like people discussing a secret, past the milestone which was about halfway, past the stile on the left —

But here, although she still had some breath and energy left, Jessica suddenly dismounted, for a quick glance had shown her that her friend, Mary Skelton, was coming along the field path on the other side of the stile.

"Hallo," she called as Mary climbed the stile. "Come and see what Cox let me have at the fish shop to-day."

Mary approached.

"My dear! Not a *whole* salmon?" She regarded the noble creature with awe. "Introduce me, will you?"

"Sir Marmaduke Middlecut — Miss Mary Skelton," replied Jessica promptly, and they both giggled. "Isn't he a beauty?"

"He certainly is. Do you think it's quite the thing to push him round the countryside all naked and unadorned like that, though?" Mary sounded critical.

"I did wrap him in paper, to begin with, but it was quite an inadequate piece, as I'd only expected cod fillets or something," Jessica explained earnestly, "and the moment I put him in the basket, he popped his head through a thin bit in the paper, and has been regarding me with a very House of Lords stare ever since."

"Oh, well, I could take more than a haughty look from a salmon I'd captured for my own table," Mary said philosophically. "Are you having it hot or cold? I never can decide which I love best."

"Cold — and to-morrow," replied Jessica promptly. "In fact, Marmaduke is almost a direct answer to prayer, for Aunt Miriam and Uncle Hector are coming to-morrow to — talk things over. And if there's one thing in the world which could move Uncle Hector to take a genial and tolerant view of life, it's cold salmon."

"How lucky." Mary was appropriately impressed. "It's very important that he *should* be put in a good mood, isn't it?"

"If it didn't sound melodramatic, I'd say our whole future depends on it," Jessica declared.

"As bad as that?" Mary thoughtfully wrinkled her very pretty nose as they began to walk on up the hill side by side. "In that case, you'd better tell the twins to run over this evening, and I'll give you a cucumber out of the greenhouse. There's one about ready, I think."

"Mary, you're an angel!"

"Not at all. I want Uncle Hector to let you all stay on at The Mead, and I'm perfectly willing to co-operate in any scheme to that end," Mary declared with emphasis. "What are the chances, Jess — of your persuading him, I mean?"

Jessica didn't reply at once, but her small oval face, with the big, dark-lashed grey eyes, looked thoughtful.

"Frankly, I don't think they're good," she said at last, with a sigh. "You see, Uncle Hector's really very much annoyed at having been made an executor of Daddy's will. He says, very truly, that he's no blood relation of the twins and me, and I think he feels it's very inconsiderate of Aunt Miriam ever to have got herself related to us."

"Even uncles by marriage must expect a few

6

family jobs of that kind occasionally," Mary retorted rather indignantly. "Why shouldn't he do it?"

"Well," Jessica explained, "I expect, to anyone of Uncle Hector's exact mind, it's specially annoying being made executor of a will where there's no money. I think he would probably have administered a ten-thousand-pound estate with fairly good grace."

"You mean he's afraid he may have to put his hand into his own pocket?" Mary suggested shrewdly.

"Yes." Jessica nodded. "And he will, so far as the education of the twins is concerned," she admitted, "unless —"

She paused so long that Mary prompted her with friendly impatience.

"Unless —?"

"Mary, if Uncle Hector would let me keep The Mead running for a year, I believe I could build up a good connection with paying guests. This isn't the most fashionable part of the Lake District, but it is one of the most beautiful, and people always want to come here again. Take Mrs. Forrest, for instance —"

She paused again, until Mary said,

"I've taken her. What about Mrs. Forrest?"

"Well, she wrote to me only this morning and asked if she and her son could come for several weeks, almost right away. And she said quite frankly that, as she knew our circumstances must have changed since Daddy's death, the arrangement would have to be a business one, and she was prepared to pay well."

"And could afford to do so?"

"Oh, undoubtedly."

"Hm, it does seem a direct pointer to the future, doesn't it?" Mary said.

"I'm hoping Uncle Hector will see it in that light," Jessica agreed.

"Well, may Marmaduke help him to do so, darling!" Mary said fervently, as she prepared to part company with Jessica and take the side road leading to the picturesque villa where she kept house for a rich and doting father.

The superficial similarity of their positions — keeping house for a widowed father — was perhaps what had first drawn Mary and Jessica to each other. But their actual circumstances could hardly have been more different.

Mary's father was a genial, moneyed man of business, with — as he expressed it — his feet very much on the ground. Mary was his only child and, since he saw in his fair pretty daughter a daily reminder of the young wife he had adored, it was his constant pleasure to pet her and indulge her to an extent which would have been ruinous to any nature less sweet and independent than Mary's.

Jessica's father, on the contrary, had been neither genial nor moneyed, and he certainly had never been a man of business in any meaning of the phrase. Except in connection with the scientific research which absorbed both his energies and all his surplus money, he was a vague, impersonal soul and a most undemonstrative father.

Of Jessica he had undoubtedly been very fond but, after the death of his wife when the twins were born, twelve years ago, he had withdrawn more and more from personal relationships. And, though he wished Tom and Judy very well whenever he remembered their existence in a more than superficial way, he seemed to feel little or no parental responsibility towards them.

While Mary's "keeping house" consisted of overseeing (very capably, it must be admitted) a small but efficient domestic staff, and in gracing her father's dinner table as a smart and well-dressed hostess, Jessica's duties were of a much more homely and strenuous variety.

She had been ten when her mother died, and from then until she was fifteen the household suffered from a succession of more or less incompetent housekeepers. Having learned by then, from bitter experience, much of what did *not* make for a happy, well-run household, Jessica decided that the time had come for a radical change.

Without much difficulty, she persuaded her father that it would be less expensive, and could hardly be more uncomfortable, to surrender the management of affairs to her admittedly inexperienced hands. And, after some agitating, experimental weeks, the household settled down to the most regular and efficient routine it had known since the death of Jessica's mother.

Now, at twenty-two, Jessica was as capable a manager as it was possible to find, and — with the assistance of one general maid, Linda, who was devoted, though somewhat rough and ready — she had made a very happy home life for her father and her young brother and sister.

Looking back on the last seven years, Jessica thought, as she came over the brow of the hill in sight of home, that it was easy to see now, in the light of possible deprivation, just how happy those years had been.

Before her lay the house which had always been home, and the thought that she and the twins were more than likely to have to leave its dear and shabby security came over her afresh, with a pang which made her catch her breath.

No one could pretend that The Mead conformed to any known school of architecture. It straggled its green and white length over an uneconomical quantity of ground, and on both sides and in front spread a richly extravagant area of lawn.

This it was the twins' particular pleasure to preserve in a condition of velvety smoothness, and they cut it with the ancient mower and rolled it with the creaking roller almost daily. No budding dandy ever shaved his chin with more loving care than the twins shaved their lawn, and, as Jessica neared the gate, the familiar "crank, cra-a-ank" of the roller could be heard.

She bit her lip, remembering that Tom and Judy were still unaware of the shadow of dispossession which lay over them. Their father's death, a month ago, had, of course, shocked them, but they were happily ignorant of the threat to everyday life which it implied. Jessica herself had been stunned when she first realised it.

Alfred Edom had never given the impression of being either a rich or a businesslike man, but the discovery that, virtually, any means he possessed had died with him had been shattering. Even now, Jessica could not accustom herself to the idea that for future guidance — and, to a great extent, for financial support — she and the twins were dependent on two people whom they hardly knew.

Uncle Hector and Aunt Miriam — their only living relatives — had never lived sufficiently near for intimacy. Nor had they been affectionate at a distance, and it was two years since Jessica had even seen them. During that time, correspondence had been limited to Christmas cards of the more austere variety, and picture postcards dispatched from holiday resorts, bearing strictly conventional phrases relating to weather and scenery.

Even Aunt Miriam had never indicated any warm affection for her brother's children. And it must indeed have been a disagreeable shock for poor Uncle Hector when he found himself called on to administer a practically non-existent estate for the benefit of a couple of nieces and a nephew in whom he had little or no interest.

At the same time, from what Jessica could remember, she thought he was the kind of man to regard unwelcome duties in a heavily conscientious light. This would probably impel him to veto any suggestion of hers that did not conform to his own highly conventional outlook.

"He'll probably want to pack the twins off to boarding school, and put me in a hostel for business girls while I learn shorthand and typing and how to do accounts," thought Jessica gloomily.

Whereas, ever since the arrival of Mrs. Forrest's letter that morning, she had been thinking more and more enthusiastically of the plan which she had just broached to Mary.

Mrs. Forrest — the wealthy widow of a man who had been a close colleague of Alfred Edom's in his younger days — had stayed at The Mead for a few days during the previous summer. On a motor tour through the Lake District, she had called to see her late husband's friend and his family, and, partly owing to some trouble with her car, partly to the fact that she liked the neighbourhood, she had remained with the Edoms for the best part of a week.

At the time, she had told Jessica — with the enthusiastic, slightly gushing air which she affected — that she would certainly return the following year. But, not until her letter that morning, had Jessica realised that Mrs. Forrest's proposed return might very well affect the family future.

As she pushed open the gate with the front wheel of her bicycle, the creaking of the roller ceased, and Tom and Judy came rushing to greet her.

They were good-looking children. Singularly alike, in a straight, brown, rather thin way. Both had wide, friendly brown eyes; intelligent, tanned little faces; and thick dark hair, which Judy wore cut almost as short as Tom's.

"You *have* been a long time!" cried Judy, with flattering inaccuracy, while Tom, who was a kind and thoughtful child, took Jessica's bicycle for her and wheeled it towards the house.

"Gosh, is that a salmon?" He inspected the bicycle's front passenger.

"Yes. I'm going to cook it this evening and we'll have it cold to-morrow, when Aunt Miriam and Uncle Hector come."

"I call that a waste," remarked Judy, who was healthily greedy and had no inhibitions about the desirability of pretending otherwise.

"I call it rather clever," retorted Tom, but he gave Jessica such a frank grin as he spoke that she decided it was not necessary to be a hypocrite and reprove him for an attitude of artless expediency which, after all, coincided pretty closely with her own.

"Why is it clever to give salmon to people we don't like?" enquired Judy, with her usual tendency to reduce a situation to rather distressingly simple terms.

"Oh, Judy! We don't exactly dislike them," Jessica

protested quickly. "We don't know them very well, that's all."

"Well, we don't like what we do know," amended Judy obligingly, but without much real improvement.

"We're going to have to like them to a point," Tom put in, and Jessica realised that he understood rather more of the situation than she had supposed. "They'll have the chief say in what happens to us in future, won't they, Jess?"

"Oh, *no!*" cried Judy in indignant protest, before Jessica could reply. "Why should they? Jessica can decide what happens to us. Can't you?" She looked at her sister anxiously.

"Not entirely, Judy. It's all rather complicated. But I hope we shall be able to find a solution which won't mean any great change for us all," Jessica said carefully. For, without wanting to alarm the children unduly, she saw that it might be as well to prepare them for the possibility of a change.

Judy had a lively imagination, and her mind immediately rushed forward to the extremity of tragedy.

"You don't mean that we might *have to leave here?*" she gasped.

"I hope not, Judy. I'm not absolutely certain."

"And does it really depend on Uncle Hector?"

"Very largely."

"Oh, gosh! He can have the whole salmon, if that's any good," Judy cried fervently.

Jessica smiled slightly as she unhooked her basket from the handlebars, so that Tom could wheel her cycle away to the shed.

"I don't know that the salmon would help to all that extent," she said. "But it may give a general air of good feeling to a difficult discussion."

Judy looked preternaturally cast down, though she would, Jessica knew, revert to an equal degree of high spirits in a very short time. It was Tom who, pausing with the bicycle, fastened on the more practical view of the situation and said,

"Jess, do we own The Mead? I mean — did Pop?"

"No," Jessica said rather carefully. "That's one of

12

the difficulties. We rent it, and the rent is a very high one for people with practically no money."

"Meaning *us?*" enquired Judy, once more defining the situation in painfully simple terms.

"Meaning us," Jessica was bound to agree.

"Who does own it, then? Mr. Furnivall?"

Jessica shook her head.

"No. Mr. Furnivall is only the agent. The real owner is Ford Onderley, who has the big house up at Oaklands.

"Oh, dear! He doesn't even live here," Judy exclaimed with a sigh.

"I don't know that that has anything to do with it," Jessica said with a smile.

"Well, I mean one can't even go and ask him to reduce the rent," Judy explained simply.

"Silly, you couldn't, anyway," Tom told her. "People don't reduce rents. They put them up. Though, as a matter of fact, Bob Parry told me they have opened up Oaklands, and that Mr. Onderley and his sister are coming to live there for the summer," he added.

"There you are, then!" cried Judy triumphantly.

"Nonsense, dear." Jessica smiled and shook her head. "It isn't as simple as all that. I'm afraid a reduction in rent wouldn't solve our difficulties for us, even if there were any question of our achieving it."

"You mean we've *got* to let Uncle Hector decide?" Judy relapsed into exaggerated gloom once more.

"I'm afraid so. But don't wallow in despair just yet, Judy," her sister advised her briskly. "I've been thinking over what we could do, and I've a suggestion to make to Uncle Hector."

"D'you mean you have a plan?" enquired Judy, with respect and also with rising spirits.

"I suppose you might call it that." Jessica laughed.

"Oh, well, then, I dare say it will be all right," Judy said much more cheerfully. "You usually know the way out of most difficulties, Jess."

And, comforted by her rather touching faith in Jessica's powers of dealing with a problematical future, she went off to complete the rolling of the lawn, while

Tom — more thoughtfully — wheeled Jessica's bicycle into the cycle shed at the back of the house.

As she went into the house, Jessica felt her responsibilities weigh upon her suddenly with exaggerated heaviness. Judy's simple belief in her power to hold back disaster made her realise afresh how little she really had to put between them all and a bare (though common-sense) future which would hold literally nothing of the life they all loved and knew.

"I've nothing to put up to Uncle Hector but a rather hare-brained scheme, backed by a casual letter from Mrs. Forrest," she thought with a sigh. "And the worst of it is that, even if I could make Uncle Hector like the scheme, it's he who would have to take the responsibility of renewing the three years' agreement for renting the house from next quarterday. *And* he'd have to find half a year's rent in advance, for I can't see that coming out of the tiny bit that is left."

It hardly seemed, at the moment, that even Marmaduke could induce Uncle Hector to take such a beautifully unpractical view of the future that he would be persuaded to do all that.

However, this was not the first crisis with which life had presented Jessica, and she had long ago learned that there was nothing to be gained by harrowing oneself with nervous anxiety beforehand. That only unfitted one for dealing with a situation when it finally arrived.

So she concentrated every effort on creating an air of pleasant competence in the house, in the hope that Uncle Hector and Aunt Miriam would thereby see for themselves that paying guests might very reasonably flock to a place where everything was so agreeable and enjoyable.

When the next morning dawned very bright and fair, Jessica felt it was definitely a point in her favour. For, though even Uncle Hector would hardly hold her responsible for the weather, there was no denying that on a fine day one may view with benevolent optimism a project which, on a wet day, appears

14

weighed down with disadvantages and reasons for objection.

With the sunlight flickering through the trees on its green-and-white exterior, The Mead, even to less prejudiced eyes than those of Jessica and the twins, might well appear beautiful. And the lawn handsomely repaid the care of Tom and Judy that morning by looking like an Elizabethan bowling green.

Surely Uncle Hector would see that almost anyone would wish to linger in this lovely spot, where one could look across the green and brown and purple hills to where mighty Helvellyn reared his noble head in the cloudy distance.

So entranced was Jessica by the beauties which awaited her prospective paying guests that, by the time her aunt and uncle arrived, just before lunch, she had almost convinced herself that they would regard her scheme, not only in a favourable light, but as a brilliant inspiration.

Neither Uncle Hector (in good but well-worn tweeds) nor Aunt Miriam (in a serviceable raincoat because she knew what one might expect in the Lake District) appeared to be people on the lookout for brilliant inspirations, it must be confessed.

They were a serious-minded, worthy couple who liked to look twice before they leapt, and then usually decided that leaping was an unwise and undesirably impulsive method of progression. They had come to middle-aged prosperity only by the exercise of rigid economy and what Aunt Miriam called "careful management" throughout their thirty years of married life. And they were proud — and justly proud — of the fact that they had never owed anyone a penny or asked for help from a soul.

Careful investment had steadily — and, in recent years, sensationally — increased their savings. So that now, in their late fifties, they found themselves, somewhat to their own surprise, comparatively wealthy people.

But the habits of years die hard. There was nothing which they did not know about saving, and hardly anything which they did know about spending. Even the purchase of the serviceable, second-hand car in which they arrived had seemed to them a piece of princely extravagance, on which they had embarked only after earnest consultation and calculation.

It was natural, therefore, that they should regard their more or less enforced duty towards their nieces and nephew in a resigned, rather than an enthusiastic, light.

However, they both greeted Jessica and the twins quite kindly, and postponed until after lunch any discussion of the painful subject of future arrangements.

Marmaduke, reclining majestically on crisp lettuce and decorated with thin slices of Skelton cucumber, certainly created an excellent impression — though Aunt Miriam did remark that salmon was "surely a terrible price just now" and that she had always regarded it as "one of the luxuries which people in our position must forgo."

Jessica hastened to say — rather untruthfully — that salmon was extremely reasonable in price in this particular district. And was very justly punished by having Aunt Miriam enquire about exact prices, and then give her a very serious little lecture on what might and what might not be regarded as reasonable by "people in our position."

"We really got it to please you and Uncle Hector," Tom explained with tact and a certain regard for truth. And the candour of this rather touched their visitors.

"Then there's nothing more to say about it, except that we're enjoying it very much," Uncle Hector said, not unkindly. "Though I wouldn't want you to think, Jessica, that your aunt and I expect or entirely approve these little extravagances."

Jessica murmured something submissive, and the meal proceeded to a successful conclusion.

Afterwards, when Jessica and Judy had cleared away, and the washing up had been abandoned to the not very tender mercies of Linda, Uncle Hector indicated that the time had come for a serious talk between himself, his wife and Jessica. So Jessica told the twins to go into the garden and — not without backward, imploring glances from Judy — they withdrew.

"Now, Jessica —" Uncle Hector took off his spectacles and began to polish them at great length. Not because they required this attention, but because he had long ago discovered that this was an excellent method of delivering long and unwelcome statements, without the unpleasant necessity of meeting the eyes of the person to whom the statement was addressed. "Now, Jessica, this is not, as you know, purely a visit of pleasure. We have to consider the very practical problem of the future of yourself and your brother and sister."

"Yes, Uncle Hector. I've been thinking things over very carefully," Jessica began eagerly, "and I can't help feeling —"

"I, too, have been thinking things over carefully," interrupted Uncle Hector, whose technique was that of a well-intentioned steam-roller, "and, as it is obvious that no one would pay a high salary to an untrained girl like you, Jessica, I think the first essential is to enter you at a good business training college. Your aunt and I are very willing to offer you a home, my dear, while you are training, though I am sure you will not think us unfriendly if I add that we could not contemplate changing our present mode of living to the extent of offering you a *permanent* home."

"Of course not," murmured Jessica, feeling they were getting a long way away from the idea of paying guests, but deciding that it was best to let Uncle Hector have his head for the moment.

"In six to nine months, if you work hard, you should be self-supporting, Jessica," her uncle continued, while Aunt Miriam nodded gravely to indicate her agreement with this estimate. "Meanwhile, since your aunt and I do not feel equal to taking two children into our household at our age, I am afraid there is no alternative but to send Tom and Judy to boarding school. This is usually an iniquitously expensive form of education," Uncle Hector admitted, with a sigh, "but I see no other way. The children would, of

17

course, spend their holidays with us," he added without enthusiasm.

"It's very good of you, Uncle Hector, to be willing to go to so much trouble and expense on our behalf," Jessica said with sincerity. "But I have got an alternative suggestion to make, and I — I've been hoping you will allow me to try the experiment."

At the word "experiment" Uncle Hector thrust out a doubtful lower lip. He preferred well-tried methods, himself, and instinctively distrusted experiments. But he replaced his now highly polished spectacles and said:

"Well, Jessica?"

"Neither the twins nor I can bear the thought of leaving here," Jessica explained a little breathlessly, "and I want you to let me keep The Mead, and I'll undertake to pay our way by taking paying guests. The children can continue at their present day schools."

"My dear Jessica! Do you mean run a boarding house — at your age?" It was Aunt Miriam who interrupted in a deeply shocked tone. "You might have — indeed, you would have — all sorts of unpleasantnesses. People who wouldn't pay their bills, men who took too much to drink."

"I didn't propose to have licensed premises, Aunt Miriam," Jessica said patiently. "And I thought if Uncle Hector would — would give me a year to work up a connection, I could do it largely on personal recommendation, so that I got the type of visitor you — one would approve of. I've already had a letter from a Mrs. Forrest who —"

"What do you mean, exactly, Jessica, by 'if I would give you a year to work up a connection'?" enquired Uncle Hector rather ponderously.

"Well, you see, I — I've hardly any capital at all." Jessica knew she was coming now to the real fence. "I don't mean that I should require any big outlay. The place is well furnished and very few things would need to be bought. But there is the question of the house."

"Which is rented at a pretty high figure, if I remember rightly," Uncle Hector said severely.

"It's not cheap," Jessica admitted desperately. "It's rented on a three years' agreement, but we've never had any difficulty about renewal in all the twenty-one years we've been here, and —"

"When is the renewal of the agreement due?" enquired Uncle Hector, taking out a pencil and note-book — which Jessica hardly knew whether to take as a hopeful sign or otherwise.

"Next quarter-day, and —"

"My dear child!" Uncle Hector closed his notebook with a snap. "Are you going to suggest that I should enter into a further three years' agreement about this most expensive house, on the strength of some idle hope of yours that you can turn the place into a boarding house? Really, Jessica, this is childish! I'm afraid you are as unpractical as your poor father," he added heavily, in a tone which said: "And see in what a mess *he* has landed us all."

"If I could persuade Mr. Onderley to extend the agreement for one year only this time —" began Jessica.

"Most unlikely," snapped Uncle Hector. "Why should he?"

Jessica didn't really know — except that so much might depend on it.

"But if I *could* persuade him, Uncle?"

"How is the rent payable? Quarterly, in advance, I suppose?"

"H-half-yearly, in advance," Jessica admitted fear-fully, and Uncle Hector's "Tch, tch, tch," was more than discouraging.

"I might get that altered, too," Jessica suggested rather wildly. "And, if I could once make a start, I *know* I could make a success of it." And before Uncle Hector could make further objections, she explained about Mrs. Forrest's letter, and even pro-duced it, as corroborative evidence.

Uncle Hector studied the letter with an unfavour-able expression, while Jessica turned to Aunt Miriam and said eagerly:

"You see, it wouldn't be necessary then for you

19

to be bothered with me, or the twins in the holidays. We should still have a home of our own and —"

"We're quite ready to do our duty towards you, Jessica," Aunt Miriam interrupted a little reprovingly. "You mustn't think you wouldn't be welcome in our home. We're not *used* to young people, of course, but —"

"And we're not used to life in London, Aunt Miriam," Jessica explained diffidently. "I — I don't think it would be very easy, either for you or us, to — to try to adjust ourselves. And I know the twins would be miserable if they were separated and at boarding school."

"Children accustom themselves to change very quickly," Aunt Miriam stated somewhat repressively. And then: "Your uncle wants to speak again."

Jessica turned eagerly to Uncle Hector once more.

"I take it, you based your whole idea on this letter, Jessica?"

"It made me see the possibilities," Jessica admitted.

"Hm. If you were twenty years older and there were not this question of three years' agreement and half a year's rent in advance, it might be worth considering." Uncle Hector rolled out the objections with melancholy emphasis, and Jessica had the impression that he would not be really sorry to have those objections removed. After all, if she *could* make a success of this venture, undoubtedly he would be relieved of some expense and much unwelcome company.

But the three years' agreement and the half year's rent in advance stuck in Uncle Hector's throat, so to speak.

"But it wouldn't represent anything like so much expense as the scheme you yourself outlined," Jessica pleaded.

"The scheme I outlined was a sound and stable one," Uncle Hector pointed out. "Your idea involves considerable risk and is dependent on some extremely debatable provisions. All the same —" He paused and cleared his throat, while Jessica's hopes rocketed.

"I *am* prepared to give your suggestion consideration."

"Oh, Uncle Hector!"

Uncle Hector raised his hand in a gesture for silence which he had seen and admired very much on the stage in his youth.

"As you know, your aunt and I are combining this visit with our summer holiday," he said. "We propose to motor on into Scotland, and shall be away about three weeks. During that time, I suggest you see this Mr. Onderley, and find out if he is willing to — er — rent the property on terms more suited to the present emergency. Then we will discuss the matter further on our return."

"And, meanwhile, I can have Mrs. Forrest and her son?" asked Jessica eagerly.

"Oh, certainly," said Uncle Hector, who had never in his life turned away a prospect of ready money. "When do they want to come?" He referred once more to the letter.

"Right away. I could wire them."

"Or send a postcard," interjected Aunt Miriam, who thought telegrams extravagant and slightly wicked.

"Anyway, their visit would be in the nature of an experiment," Uncle Hector admitted. "If it were successful, Jessica, *and* you have a satisfactory talk with Mr. Onderley, who must, I suppose, have known you since you were a child, then I should begin to think there was something in your idea."

Not until then did Jessica realise how much was to depend on her interview with Mr. Onderley.

She opened her lips to admit that she had never met him in her life, since, until now, he had left the management of his local property in his agent's hands. But the wording of Uncle Hector's last speech suddenly recurred to her, and she closed her lips again on the untruthful implication that Mr. Onderley was a dear old gentleman who *had* known her since appealing childhood days.

No doubt this was why Uncle Hector had left her to deal with the Mr. Onderley interview. If he had known that she was as much a stranger to him as Uncle Hector himself . . .

But he did not know. And Jessica contrived to bring the visit to an agreeable and safe conclusion without either her uncle or her aunt suspecting the truth.

When they had finally driven away — at a decorous pace which Uncle Hector considered proper to his dignity and Aunt Miriam to his standard of driving — Jessica told the panting twins the gist of the interview. She considered that any anxiety about the future would be tempered for them by hopes of success, and, if they should fail in their project, at least Uncle Hector's own proposals would not come as a complete shock. Besides, they were good children, and would undoubtedly promise their quite valuable co-operation.

This they did, with whoops of excitement and optimism from Judy. Tom, more soberly, put his finger on the weak spot and said:

"It all depends on Mr. Onderley, really, doesn't it?"

"Well, a good deal depends on him," Jessica admitted.

"Bob Parry says he's a hard man," stated Tom with regretful authority.

"Bob Parry doesn't know anything about him," replied Jessica sharply, because this intelligence frightened her and she didn't want to show that it did. "He's only two years older than you."

"But his mother keeps a shop," Tom said elliptically. And Jessica mentally admitted that this vastly increased Bob's probable supply of local gossip.

"It'll be all right," Judy asserted. "Jessica will talk him round. Mr. Onderley, I mean, not Bob. When are you going to see him, Jess?"

"In a day or two. I want to settle the question of the Forrests first," said Jessica, who felt that two paying guests in hand — and probably well-paying, at that — would improve her position.

So a telegram was despatched, and Mrs. Forrest — who, unlike Uncle Hector and Aunt Miriam, delighted to leap almost before looking — replied that she and her son, David, might be expected within the next couple of days.

This set the twins frantically rolling the lawn afresh, and Jessica and — less enthusiastically — Linda making every preparation for the comfort and pleasure of their first important guests.

The result was that, by the time the Forrests arrived, on the evening of the second day, The Mead was in a condition to face a stiff military inspection, rather than the tolerant, easily-satisfied demands of Mrs. Forrest and her son.

They had driven from London during the day — in a silver-grey touring car, of dimensions and luxuriousness which would have made Uncle Hector's homely chariot look like salvage. The occupants, too, could hardly have differed more from The Mead's most recent visitors.

At fifty, Evelyn Forrest still contrived to look a very pretty woman of thirty-nine and, in her expensive motoring coat and deceptively simple hat, she would not have disgraced the pages of an exclusive fashion journal.

She kissed Jessica and the twins and then introduced the tall, fair young man with her.

"This is my boy, David, Jessica. I'm afraid he *is* an artist, but not a very arty one. I mean, he does portraits."

"What my mother really means is that I contrive to sell my work at high prices," David Forrest explained with a smile. "And that's either an advantage or an affront to art for art's sake — just as you care to look at it."

"I should call it an advantage," Jessica said as she shook hands with him and smiled.

She decided she was going to like David Forrest. For one thing, his handgrip was firm, and, for another, he didn't seem at all embarrassed by the puppyish friendliness of the twins.

There was nothing of the flowing tie or luxuriant hair convention about him. In fact, he looked the regulation sportsman, if he looked the regulation anything, except for the fact that he had inherited from his mother rather romantically long, dark lashes, which did not, Jessica thought, detract at all from the general charm.

"Darling, I think the place is looking even *more* beautiful than before. Though, of course, one misses your dear father," said Mrs. Forrest, recollecting that, even if she were not missing him, she ought to be. "But I'm sure you manage everything perfectly."

"Well, I hope I'm going to manage it to your satisfaction," Jessica told her with a smile, while Judy said very literally:

"Anyway, Daddy never had anything to do with the managing. Jess always did it."

" 'Always' can't have been a very long time, judging from Jess's youthful appearance," declared David.

But Judy was quite ready and willing to put that right.

"Oh, yes. Jessica has looked after everything since she was fifteen, and she's twenty-two now," she announced obligingly.

"You keep the family secrets to yourself," David said. But he smiled at Jessica in a way that expressed frank admiration without any hint of boldness.

And Jessica reflected that the taking of paying guests was going to have its pleasure, as well as its profit.

During the next few days, life at The Mead proceeded with a smoothness beyond Jessica's most optimistic hope. Evelyn Forrest was good-tempered and unexacting, and, provided one noticed — and even sometimes remarked — how really nice she was, she was very easy to please.

David, too, was easy-going — with a nice sense of humour which was somewhat lacking in his mother. He was also a good deal more observant and, while she constantly said that she wondered how Jessica contrived to do so much work and still look decorative, he was not at all above lending a hand in the garden, and even in the house, if necessary.

To Jessica, it seemed that she could hardly have had two more ideal guests with which to start her venture. And when, after a day or two, everything seemed in good running order, she decided that the time had come to make her rather frightening appeal to Mr. Onderley.

At first, she thought of telephoning and asking for an appointment. But, on second thoughts, she decided that an informal, semi-neighbourly call might produce better results. So, choosing that indefinite time between tea and dinner, when most people can be relied on to be at home, Jessica set out for Oaklands, the big house, standing in a small, well-kept park, which lay about half a mile beyond the Skeltons' place.

With shameless guile, she had chosen her most becoming outfit, for — hard man and crusty old curmudgeon though he might be — Mr. Onderley would not be less likely to yield because one was easy to look at.

In her well-cut grey suit, Jessica knew she looked graceful, and as near tall as she was ever likely to look. And the almost copper-coloured silk blouse and gloves were the exact shade of her hair, which she dressed on top of her head in a shining coronet. Unlike the twins, Jessica had clear grey eyes, but the lashes were dark enough to give the illusion of almost dark eyes and, whereas at this time of year the twins achieved a rich brown tan, Jessica's fine, pale skin took nothing more than a warm, golden shade.

It was probable that at least half Uncle Hector's misgivings about her capabilities for running any venture of her own were due to the fact that his niece was an extraordinarily pretty girl. Jessica, while vaguely aware of this, presumed to hope that Mr. Onderley's reactions would be different.

As she passed the Skelton's house, Mary, who saw her from a window, ran out to the gate to speak to her.

"Hallo, darling. What are you doing, passing an old friend like this?"

Jessica smiled and stopped.

"I'm going up to Oaklands, to have it out with Mr. Onderley," she explained. "Don't uncross your fingers once all the time I'm away."

"Jess! Are you really going?" Mary — who had, of course, had a full account of the interview with

Uncle Hector — looked half amused and half anxious.

"Certainly. Why not?"

"Well — don't pin too many hopes to it, dear. I hear he is very much the hard landlord of fiction," Mary said doubtfully.

"I've got to pin all my hopes to it." Jessica spoke almost violently. "If he won't agree to alter the terms of the agreement — it's business college for me and boarding school for the children."

"Well, all the luck in the world, Jess," Mary said heartily.

"She sounded as though she thought I'd need it," reflected Jessica a little grimly as she went on.

Oaklands was much the biggest and the most beautiful house in the neighbourhood, dating from considerably more than a hundred years ago and combining the elegance of the best Regency period with the rich solidity of early Victorianism.

This was the first time Jessica had approached nearer than the gate of the small park, and her heart beat with mingled excitement and nervousness as she walked up the drive and boldly pulled the big brass bell-pull which hung at the side of the front door.

At the same moment, the door opened — too quickly for it to have been in answer to Jessica's ring — to disclose a slim, elegant, dark-haired girl about half a dozen years older than Jessica herself. She was in a very lovely jade green evening dress, over which she wore a short mink cape, and she was obviously going out.

As Jessica stood aside to let her pass, she gave a faint, rather remote smile and said,

"Good evening. Did you want to see someone?"

"Yes. If Mr. Onderley is in, I'd like to see him for a few minutes," explained Jessica, feeling not quite so tall and not half so smartly dressed as she had felt five minutes ago.

"Yes, he's in. Barden" — she spoke over her shoulder to a manservant who was now hovering in the background — "this lady wants to see Mr. Onderley."

And, with a little nod, she went down the steps

to a big closed car which had just driven round from the side of the house.

"That must be his daughter," thought Jessica as she followed the manservant across the hall and into a high, panelled room, where wide bay windows gave a beautiful view across the valley at the back of the house.

"The name is Miss Edom," Jessica explained. "I haven't got an appointment with Mr. Onderley, but if he could spare me a few minutes, I'd be very glad."

It was no longer sounding at all like an informal, semi-neighbourly call, she realised. But the servant's rather unbending attitude seemed to indicate that that would have been out of place in any case.

He went away, and Jessica was left alone, a good deal oppressed by the silence and the magnificence of the place. In the friendly, familiar surroundings of The Mead, it had not seemed very unreasonable to come and lay her difficulties before her unknown land-lord. At the gate of Mary Skelton's home it had begun to seem a trifle bold. In this quiet, luxurious room, the idea appeared presumptuous and quite ter-rifyingly impossible of execution.

"Don't be silly! He can't eat you," she admonished herself. "And, even if he is the kind of horrid old thing who shouts, he must have his softer moments. That daughter of his was never dressed by an un-bendingly stern papa."

But none of this reassured her very much and, when she heard a step in the hall outside, Jessica rose to her feet with an odd sensation of not being able to breathe very easily. If he were big and bully-ing . . .

The door opened, and into the room came a tall, dark, extremely good-looking man in a riding suit, and, at a bewildered, hasty guess, Jessica put his age at something like thirty.

"I wanted to see Mr. Onderley," she explained, with more of a gasp than she had intended. "Mr. Ford Onderley."

"Yes?" he said. "What can I do for you? I am Ford Onderley."

CHAPTER TWO

JESSICA opened her eyes very wide and said, "Are you *really?*" before she could quite check her astonishment.

Then she blushed, felt some apology was due, and hastily stammered:

"I — I beg your pardon. I didn't think — I mean, you aren't at all as I expected you to be."

He looked amused, as though he thought her gauche — which no doubt he did — and Jessica felt she was not conducting this interview very skilfully.

"Won't you sit down?" He indicated a chair, into which she rather thankfully subsided. "What can I do for you, Miss Edom? I believe you are quite a near neighbour of mine, aren't you?"

It was nice of him, Jessica thought passingly, to refer to her as a neighbour, rather than a tenant, and, recovering herself a little, she said,

"Yes. I live up at The Mead with my young brother and sister. As a matter of fact, you're our landlord," she added a trifle naïvely.

"As a matter of fact, I believe I am," he agreed, looking amused again. "I think Furnivall spoke about you. Didn't you lose your father very recently?"

"Yes, we did."

"I'm sorry about that," he said, conventionally, but quite pleasantly. "Both for you and for myself. I understand I lost a very excellent tenant in him."

This seemed as good an opening as any, so, gripping her hands together with a nervous tension which was not lost on her host, Jessica boldly plunged with:

"It was about the renewal of the tenancy that I wanted to speak to you, Mr. Onderley."

"Oh, yes?" He turned his chair slightly, and she wondered if it were only a trick of the light which made her think that his mouth hardened. That, and the remembered warnings of Bob Parry and Mary.

"I expect you know," she explained rather breathlessly, "that our three-yearly agreement is renewable

28

next quarter-day, and that the rent is payable half-yearly in advance?"

He nodded, to indicate that he knew, as well as Jessica, the terms on which his property was rented.

"Well, I came to ask if you would consider making the agreement a yearly one and — and the rent payable *quarterly* in adv —"

"Not without very good reason, Miss Edom," he interrupted, so unequivocally that she winced. But she returned eagerly to the attack.

"There *is* a very good reason," she began.

"From your point of view, or mine?"

"Well — well, ours," she admitted. "But if you don't mind hearing about it in detail —?"

He made a slight gesture for her to proceed, though neither his extremely observant dark eyes nor his over-firm mouth relaxed into any smile of encouragement.

However, with or without encouragement, the story must be told, and, in as steady a voice as she could achieve, Jessica explained about their changed financial position. Uncle Hector's worthy but somewhat dreary proposals for the future, and her own counter-proposal and her uncle's reception of it.

He heard her through to the end, quite patiently. Then, as her voice died away into what she found distinctly embarrassing silence, he regarded her speculatively and said:

"Your uncle is not averse to this paying guest proposition, as such? Only if he is himself involved in any financial risk?"

"Yes, exactly." Jessica wondered if his thoughtful tone meant that he was considering the position.

"And your proposal is that any financial risks should therefor be shifted from his shoulders to mine?"

Jessica blushed at the dryness of his tone.

"Well, I — there wouldn't be very much risk for you, Mr. Onderley."

"On the contrary, I have a very desirable tenant anxious to take on The Mead at an increased rental," he informed her coolly. "Alternatively, I could sell the place at an excellent price. Your suggestion —

if carried out — would mean that I rejected two good certainties, for the speculative pleasure of watching you experiment in something in which you have no experience — my rent being dependent on the success of the experiment, incidentally."

"The — the rent is payable in advance," Jessica reminded him in a greatly subdued tone. "You'd be sure of that, anyway."

"It would be a little difficult to throw you all out, halfway through the year, because of non-payment of rent," he informed her. "Particularly as I feel sure you would come and plead your cause with at least as much eloquence as on this occasion."

Jessica flushed angrily.

"You think I'm cadging, don't you? Just because I come here and ask for easier terms in — in the present emergency."

"No, not necessarily. I'm thinking how very shrewd it was of your Uncle Hector to let you come and do the pleading," was the rather unexpected reply.

A small, uncontrollable smile flitted over Jessica's face.

"Well, you see, he — he had the idea that you'd known me since I was young enough to pat on the head."

"And thought that my hard heart was more likely to melt to the pleas of my little favourite than to the arguments of an Uncle Hector?" finished Ford Onderley, with a grim smile in his turn.

"S-something like that," Jessica confessed.

"A view in which, I notice, you seem to have concurred, since you left him in ignorance of his mistake."

"Well, I thought I'd do it better than Uncle Hector," Jessica explained earnestly. "After all, my heart's more in it. He would only be discussing an arrangement which would suit his convenience. *I'm* talking about the happiness and home of myself and the twins."

"How old are the twins?" he enquired — irrelevantly, she thought.

"Twelve."

"Ah, I see. Not of a sufficiently tender age to add

pathos to the situation, and so you didn't bring them with you."

Jessica jumped to her feet, scarlet with the angry certainty that he was finding this interview no more than mildly amusing.

"I'm sorry — I shouldn't have come," she cried, and it annoyed her still further to find that her voice was shaking. "I ought to have been warned. Mary said it wouldn't be any good, and that I mustn't hope you'd —"

"Sit down," he interrupted coolly. "We're still discussing the possibilities of your plan, you know. Only, I have no intention of being imposed on by you or Uncle Hector. Nor do I intend to bolster up any project which is doomed from the start by incompetence."

"But I — I'm not incompetent. Really I'm not." Jessica spoke more quietly.

"No?" He smiled, and, for the first time, it was not an unkindly smile. "You don't strike me as incompetent, I admit, even though you are so extremely young and lovely. But I can't take your competence entirely on trust, you know. Tell me something more about your plan of action, for I never lend my support to any venture without knowing all about it — flinty-hearted though that may seem to you and — Mary."

Jessica sat down slowly again, glanced at her host, and took heart from the fact that there was an undoubted glint of amusement in his eyes. Nothing tolerant in his expression — but at least he was ready to listen.

So she carefully explained about the promising beginning she had made with the Forrests, and how she intended to build up a good connection, as far as possible by personal recommendation.

"Provided you achieve something worth recommending, I might be able to help you there," he said unexpectedly.

"Oh, Mr. Onderley!" Hope leapt into Jessica's shining eyes. "Do you mean you're considering my proposition?"

31

"Certainly I'm considering it. You don't suppose I should be wasting so much time on it if I didn't think it was possibly worthy of support, do you?"

"Oh, I'm sorry I was rude to you," cried Jessica with contrition. "I was scared and — and so much depended on it. I'm not really taking your support for granted, you know. It's most awfully good of you —"

"Please don't rush from one extreme to the other," he begged. "It's really rather embarrassing to be credited with a cloven hoof one moment and a halo the next, you know." But he looked amused, and not at all embarrassed. "I'm really neither a villain nor a philanthropist. The point is that your father was always an excellent tenant of mine. There is therefore no reason why I should not be reasonably accommodating in what you so engagingly term 'the present emergency,' provided —"

"It was Uncle Hector's phrase — not mine," murmured Jessica.

"My respect for Uncle Hector increases," remarked Ford Onderley ironically. "But, as I was saying, there is no reason why I should not help you, provided I find that you are sufficiently capable and hard-working to deserve help."

"You mean you've no use for duds, however unfortunate?" suggested Jessica with a little grin which was entirely devoid of rancour.

"I mean, my dear," he said dryly, "that it is singularly easy in this wicked world for the lazy to pass themselves off as the unfortunate, and every day it is being made easier for them. I don't intend to facilitate matters still further. In fact, to return from the general to the particular, my willingness to help you depends very much on your willingness to help yourself."

"Well, that's fair," Jessica agreed heartily. "And, though I dare say I sounded resentful and touchy at first, I don't in the least mind your doing a bit of personal investigating. In fact" — she smiled at him winningly — "you'd better come and see us for yourself."

"Is that a direct invitation?" He too smiled.

"Of course."

"When may I come?"

"This evening," Jessica said promptly. "Then you'll know things haven't been specially prepared for you."

"Not afraid to be taken unawares, eh?" He looked amused but approving. "Well, I call that a good suggestion. Do you really mean that I may call some time this evening?"

"No. I mean — will you come back to dinner with me?" Jessica replied, her colour rising a little with excitement and a sort of heady enjoyment of her own boldness.

"My dear child, that's really very nice of you."

"And rather good technique, don't you think?" Jessica could not quite resist.

He paid that the tribute of a laugh.

"And very good technique," he agreed. "I accept — with real pleasure."

"Good!" Jessica said. Then she remembered the lovely woman in the green evening dress, who could certainly not be his daughter and was therefore probably his wife. "I suppose you *would* really prefer to do that, rather than wait until Mrs. Onderley can come too? She might be a more searching critic, being a woman."

"I'm afraid we should have to wait too long," he explained gravely. "There is no Mrs. Onderley, nor any prospect of one at the moment."

"Oh!" Jessica laughed at his way of putting it. "I thought — There was someone coming out of the house as I came in, and I assumed she was Mrs. Onderley."

"I expect it was my sister, Angela. She lives here with me and runs the place," he explained briefly. "Do you mind waiting ten minutes while I change?"

"No. Of course not."

"You'll find the evening papers on that table, and I'll send Barden in with drinks."

When he had gone, Jessica got up and walked softly up and down the room. She felt too excited to sit still, and certainly much too excited to read evening newspapers.

She had succeeded! At least, she had almost succeeded, and the rest depended on her being able to prove herself. She felt elated and on her mettle. And suddenly she found that she vastly preferred Ford Onderley's astringent and critical analysis of the situation to any sentimental and indiscriminate aid, applied without enquiry.

"If he does help me, I shan't feel it's a sort of charity. Just the sort of obligation which one self-respecting person may accept from another because of" — she chuckled as she recalled the phrase — "a temporary emergency."

As she wandered about the handsome room, she noted with interest the furnishing, the choice of books lying about (his or his sister's?) and, finally, an excellent studio photograph of Angela.

This Jessica studied at some length — more perhaps for the superficial likeness to her host than for the intrinsic interest of the photograph.

Like her brother, Angela Onderley had wide-set dark eyes, a straight, almost classical nose, and extremely good bone structure. There, Jessica thought, the real likeness ended. For though, in each case, the mouth was unusually firm, Angela's lips were fine, to the point of thinness, while his, Jessica had noted, were full, generous, possibly even a trifle sensual. Angela's hair, too — even allowing for the artistic licence of a studio portrait — was soft and fine and cloudy. His was thick and strong, and grew with that curious suggestion of aggressiveness which is seen only in people of tremendous vitality.

On the whole, an interesting personality, thought Jessica. Interesting and, in some indefinable way, exciting. Quite possibly he *was* hard, as people said, but it was a good, sound hardness.

"Not like a stone," reflected Jessica, "but like a good, hard apple." Then she laughed aloud at her own simile, and, at that moment, he came back into the room.

"Well, what's the joke?" he wanted to know, as he poured out sherry for them both.

"Oh, n-nothing. Just something rather silly I thought of," Jessica said, blushing as she took her glass from him.

"Something about me," he suggested, noting the blush, she felt sure. "Has the hard-hearted landlord degenerated so rapidly into a mere joke?"

"Oh, *no!*"

"Still the hard-hearted landlord, eh?"

"No. At least" — and then she laughed again — "that was really what made me laugh. I was thinking that, even if you are hard, it's a nice, healthy hardness. Not like a stone, but like a good, hard apple."

"I see." He gave her an extremely quizzical smile as he drank off the rest of his sherry. "May I enquire if you intend to set your teeth in the good, hard apple?"

"Do I look as though I bite?" returned Jessica with a quick flash of amusement.

"A little — yes, when you're angry," was the unexpected retort. "Come along. I'll run you down home by car."

Smiling rather at their final exchange of words, Jessica accompanied him out of the room.

Outside, in the drive, a car was waiting. Not the sumptuous saloon car which had taken Angela to her evening appointment, but a small racing car.

"Do you mind an open car?" he asked.

"No," Jessica said. "Nor a bicycle, nor even my own legs, if necessary."

"Accommodating girl," he replied with an air which said that he found her rather pert.

"It's not really a case of being accommodating," Jessica explained more earnestly. "I've not had enough to do with cars to turn choosy about them."

"I see," he said, and held the low door open for her.

It was astonishingly comfortable, Jessica found, though obviously built for speed first and foremost, and she was glad that — possibly in deference to her inexperienced nerves — he chose to drive at a very reasonable pace.

As they passed the Skeltons' house, Mary, who was in the front garden, looked up, registered a gratifying degree of astonishment at seeing Jessica actually driving past with the dragon, and waved her hand in mingled salutation and congratulation.

Jessica was unable to resist waving back with a certain air of complacent triumph, and — possibly noting the quality of her smile — her companion enquired:

"A friend of yours?"

"Yes. That's Mary Skelton. Her father —"

"Ah, the young lady who thinks so badly of me?"

"Oh, she doesn't really, Mr. Onderley. She doesn't know anything about you," Jessica cried earnestly.

"That wouldn't necessarily prevent her thinking badly of me," was the slightly cynical reply. "At least she thought you would be wasting your time by coming to see me, didn't she?"

"Oh, well — no, not really. She'd just heard you were rather the hard landlord of fiction, you know," explained Jessica, and then wondered if she had made things sound any better. "You mustn't mind if people say rather idiotic things before they get to know you. They always do in a place this size, you'll find. Why, we were known as a 'theatrical' family for years, just because my mother let me and my friends dress up and invent plays in the garden on Saturday afternoons."

"Thank you. You make me feel much better about it," he said with extreme gravity. Whereat Jessica blushed and wondered if he usually found people amusing, or just found her specially so.

On their arrival at The Mead, the twins came out to greet the extraordinary spectacle of their sister returning with the spoils of war in the shape of Mr. Onderley himself.

"I say, it was nice of you to come down and see us for yourself," Tom said as he shook hands. While Judy — in much the same words, but with even more frankness than her sister — added:

"We didn't think you'd be a bit like this."

"Will someone tell me what you did expect me to

be like?" their visitor said with real curiosity.

"Oh, yes," Judy explained obligingly. "We thought you'd be old and cross, with fuzzy eyebrows and a barking voice. At least, I did."

"Did you think I'd be like that?" enquired Ford Onderley gravely, turning to Jessica.

"N-not exactly," Jessica said, a little put out. Then she added hastily: "Would you like to see around your own property? Because, if so, the children will take you round while I see about dinner."

"Yes, do come," Judy begged, and took him by the hand, which seemed to astonish him a good deal.

However, he went off with the twins with quite a good grace, and Jessica ran into the house to give the finishing touches to the dinner, since this could be left to Linda only in the initial stages.

"I don't reckon to do fancy touches," was one of Linda's favourite sayings, and she could hardly have reckoned more accurately.

As Jessica was passing through the hall, she saw David Forrest coming down the stairs, and, on sudden impulse, she decided to enlist his aid.

"I say, will you be a special angel to-night?" she begged. "I mean — be very scintillating and entertaining at dinner, will you? I've invited my landlord to dinner, and I want to give him the general impression that The Mead is the abode of wit and learning and good food."

David Forrest leaned over the banisters to smile at her and catch her half-whispered, urgent plea.

"I'll do my best," he promised. "What are his special interests?"

"I can't imagine. The Stock Exchange, I should think, for one."

"I can't possibly scintillate about the Stock Exchange," David Forrest stated firmly. "But I'll do my best with what might be termed general subjects. Do you want any help? With the dinner, I mean?"

"Good heavens, no! Though thank you very much. I don't know many men who'd offer to give a hand with a meal. But, anyway, that wouldn't do at all. I want him to recommend this place to his distinguished friends, and he certainly wouldn't if he thought they were expected to cream the potatoes or make the salad dressing."

"They might enjoy it," remarked David Forrest argumentatively.

"Oh, no!"

"Why not — if I should?"

"Because I can't possibly expect many of them to be as nice as you," Jessica said simply.

Then she went off into the kitchen, leaving him to look after her with a very reflective smile and a slightly heightened colour. And presently he went out into the garden to join the twins and their visitor.

While Jessica rapidly put the finishing touches to the dinner, she mentally decided that, whereas it had been good technique to take David into her confidence, it would be a mistake to say anything to Mrs. Forrest.

She entered into everything with such gusto that she would undoubtedly overplay her part, and make Mr. Onderley suspicious by virtue of the sheer lavishness of her praise. Mrs. Forrest was, in all genuineness, what advertisements call a highly satisfied client, and could be left to show her pleasure and enthusiasm without any prompting or appeals.

It was nice of David to respond so whole-heartedly to her plea, Jessica thought with a grateful smile. And, glancing out of a side window, she saw that, even now, he was strolling up and down the lawn in conversation with Ford Onderley — thus rescuing him from an overdose of the twins' society before the novelty of their friendliness could degenerate into boredom over their juvenile enthusiasm.

Only at that moment did Jessica recall, with full comprehension, the frankness with which she had given David her opinion of himself. Really, it had been rather forthcoming of her after only a week's acquaintance!

But, somehow, one felt like that with David. (Characteristically, one already thought of him as David.) Besides, why shouldn't he know that he and his mother were the ideal paying guests?

By the time the two men came in to dinner, they

seemed on very sociable terms, and Judy found an occasion to whisper to her sister that Mr. Onderley was "quite all right, and not so difficult to talk to as Uncle Hector," from which Jessica dared to hope that the twins, in their turn, had made a fairly favourable impression.

Conversation never languished in any company which included Mrs. Forrest, and Jessica thought it was almost amusing to hear how naturally she gravitated from discussing the beauties of the neighbourhood to praise of life at The Mead.

"Of course, we're specially lucky in having such a pleasant place to stay," she explained to Ford Onderley. "Jessica runs this house beautifully. I'm going to recommend her to *all* my friends. I always tell her that I don't know how she manages to be so capable and so decorative at the same time."

"It certainly is an achievement," agreed their visitor gravely, with a little bow in Jessica's direction, which somehow made her feel that he was quite as amused as she, at the unrehearsed effect of Mrs. Forrest's praise.

"When you paint Jessica, will you have her looking capable or looking decorative?" Judy asked David Forrest at this point. At which Jessica looked a good deal surprised, and David a little put out.

"I haven't even asked her if I *may* paint her yet, Judy," David said with a frown. "And now you've crushed all my plans for a diplomatic approach."

"Can't you just ask without being diplomatic?" Judy suggested, and they all laughed.

"Well, Jessica, you see it's out of my hands." David smiled at her. "Without diplomacy, may I ask you across your own dinner table — will you sit for me some time?"

"Decoratively or capably?" enquired Jessica, looking amused.

"We'll decide on that afterwards."

"Couldn't you do her making pastry?" enquired Judy. "She's got a very pretty greeny-grey overall, and she'd look both capable *and* decorative then."

"It's an idea!" declared Mrs. Forrest, ignoring her

39

son's rather annoyed expression. "And then, if it were one of David's most successful portraits, it might be in the Academy. How would you like that, Judy — to have your sister's portrait in the Academy?"

"It'd be marvellous," agreed Judy enthusiastically. "And p'raps a millionaire would see it and fall in love with her and buy it."

Everyone laughed, except David, who said shortly.

"It wouldn't be for sale. Will you really sit for me, Jessica?"

"Yes, of course, if you want me to." Jessica smiled at him, and thought it was quite extraordinarily officious of Ford Onderley to murmur:

"Will such a busy person have sufficient time?"

"I'll fit it in somehow," Jessica assured him with a little toss of her head, and hoped he understood thereby that even if he were entitled to inform himself on the efficiency with which she ran her home, he was certainly not at liberty to query her use of her own time.

He accepted the rebuke with a rather quizzical glance, but turned almost immediately to David to say:

"I know your work quite well and, if I may say so, I've always admired it. Are you strictly on holiday here? Except for the proposed study of Miss Edom, I mean?"

"Well" — David smiled — "I can't say an artist is ever strict about holidays. If I saw a subject I wanted to paint, I shouldn't bother about being on holiday."

"You must come over and meet my sister." Ford Onderley spoke abruptly, like a man who saw no point in wasting time on a detailed approach to his subject. "I should very much like to have you do a portrait of her, if you're interested in the commission."

"That's very kind of you. I should be happy to meet your sister, of course," David said, but a trifle remotely. And Jessica had the impression that he preferred to choose his own subjects, rather than accept a commission just because someone was willing to pay well.

She would have been less than human if she had not been gratified by the implication, and she gave David the very nicest smile of which she was capable.

After dinner the twins went to bed — with an almost unnatural docility and lack of protest, since they, too, wished to contribute all they could to the general good impression which Mr. Onderley was to receive — and Jessica served her guests with admirable coffee in the long, pleasant lounge which looked over the garden.

She felt a little like a hard-working student who had sat for a stiff examination, fondly believed she had done well, but still awaited the results with some trepidation. And when Ford Onderley finally rose to go, she accompanied him to the gate with an air of hopeful expectancy which she could not suppress, though she knew it was more suited to one of Judy's age and temperament than her own.

Perhaps he found it a little touching, as well as amusing, because, as they went down the path together towards the gate, he took her lightly and rather kindly by her arm.

"You're putting up a very good fight, Jessica," he said. "May I call you Jessica?"

"Yes," she said, though she was slightly startled by the suggestion. "Everyone calls me Jessica, so you can, too."

"Thank you."

"Did you mean — just now — that you do think you'll help me, by letting me have the tenancy on easier terms?" she asked eagerly, because she could not bear to be kept in suspense any longer.

"Yes," he said slowly. "I've been thinking over the best way to arrange it. You can have the tenancy on a yearly agreement."

"And the rent quarterly in advance?" she prompted hopefully.

"No. The rent annually — in arrear."

"But —" She stopped dead, and perforce he had to stop too. "What do you mean, quite?"

"That you can go through this coming year without paying rent for The Mead," he explained calmly.

"If, at the end of the year, you have made a good profit and look like succeeding, you can pay your year's rent and renew your tenancy. If, in spite of hard work, you have the misfortune to fail, I will not add to your burden by expecting you to pay the year's rent. Is that clear?"

"Qu-quite clear," gasped Jessica, so moved by his totally unexpected generosity that she felt ridiculously like crying. "It's most terribly kind of you. I — I don't know what to say."

"Then you needn't say anything," he told her. "You might just mention to Mary Skelton that I have my softer moments, however."

"Oh, I will," cried Jessica fervently. "Indeed I will. But you mustn't think Mary meant anything serious. She's the sweetest person, really, and no one will be better pleased than she to hear how nice you really are."

He laughed — perhaps at the naïve implication.

"Well, you must both come over to Oaklands soon and meet Angela," he said, with what Jessica could not help feeling was a touch of masculine obtuseness. Angela, if she were not much mistaken, was a young lady who chose her own friends.

But aloud she said:

"Thank you. That will be lovely." And stood by, smiling beatifically, as he got into his car.

Then, just as she thought he was preparing to drive away, and she herself was going to say goodbye, he leant forward and said:

"May I ask something which is not at all my business?"

"Yes — if you like."

"Has young Forrest some idea that he's in love with you?"

Jessica opened her eyes very wide, until they shone, clear grey, between their dark lashes.

"I shouldn't think so. Whatever made you ask?"

"I don't want him to get any such idea — that's all. Good night."

And, with a smile and a little nod to her, he drove away.

CHAPTER THREE

FOR QUITE a long time after Ford Onderley had driven away, Jessica stood leaning her arms on the gate and looking out across the countryside, from which the last gleams of daylight were fading.

What had he meant by that last curious question and comment?

Did he presume to disapprove of David? Or to suggest that she would have no time for romantic side lines if she were to do her job thoroughly? Or could he possibly mean that he, personally, preferred not to have another man interested in her?

But the last suggestion was so ridiculous, on the strength of one evening's acquaintance, that Jessica dismissed it with a smile. And, finally deciding that this was just one side of her unpredictable landlord which she did not yet understand, she went back into the house, to receive the amused congratulations of David and Mrs. Forrest.

"David's just been explaining to me, dear, that we were all more or less on probation this evening," Mrs. Forrest said. "I do hope we all passed the test all right."

"With honours," Jessica assured her, with a laugh. "Though *you* weren't exactly on probation, you know. Only in so far as you were subjects for demonstration."

"But we did *help*, I hope."

"I'll say you did!" Jessica declared gratefully. "Your unrehearsed tributes were just what were required."

"I do wish I'd known beforehand what was happening. I'd have said so *much* more," Mrs. Forrest said regretfully.

"Then you'd have painted the lily out of all recognition, Mama dear," her son assured her. "It was much nicer as it was."

"But you knew, didn't you?"

"Yes, but that's different. I'm a born diplomat," David explained complacently.

"You weren't very diplomatic over painting Jessica's portrait," his mother reminded him.

"That was Judy's fault," David declared. "But you are going to let me do it, aren't you, Jessica?" He turned to her eagerly.

"Of course. I'm flattered. I gathered you don't paint just — anyone who wants to be painted."

"Oh, you mean the lord of the manor's precious sister?" David dismissed her with a scornful gesture.

"She's quite lovely, David."

"Very likely," said David with supreme indifference. "He's quite a good-looking beggar himself. Is she like him?"

"Yes. She is rather. Not quite so much character, I should say."

"But then a woman doesn't need so much character as a man, does she?" Mrs. Forrest said. And, as neither of her hearers could either agree with her or bring themselves to voice their dissent in sufficiently restrained terms, the subject was dropped.

The next few days were the happiest Jessica had experienced since the death of her father and the realisation of their changed circumstances.

Most of her anxieties had been removed. That is to say, the helpless feeling of having her future and that of the twins taken out of her hands had now gone. If hard work and reasonably good fortune could keep them independent, then independent they would remain.

Curbing her enthusiasm and her optimism within reasonable bounds, she wrote to her uncle and aunt, explaining in terms of great moderation the success of her interview with Ford Onderley, and received in return a cautious letter of commendation from her uncle.

In the same envelope (because, after all, there was no need to waste another stamp) was a note from her aunt, stating that the weather was changeable, but they were enjoying the scenery, and she hoped that dear Jessica would not *count her chickens before they were hatched*.

"I suppose she regards future prospective paying

guests as the unhatched chickens," Jessica said to Mary when she was giving her a full account of all that had happened.

"No doubt. But I detect a note of relief in both letters, don't you?" remarked Mary thoughtfully.

"Oh, yes. It's natural enough, you know." Jessica smiled. "The poor old dears are completely set in their ways, and I'm sure it was only the strongest sense of duty that urged them to offer something like a home to me and the twins. They'd have hated it quite as much as we should. I think it was rather sweet of them even to make the offer, in the circumstances."

"Of course. But now," said Mary, thoughtfully and wickedly, "thanks to the magnanimity of the harsh Mr. Onderley, everyone is happy."

"He's really rather a darling when you get to know him, Mary," Jessica protested.

"Nonsense, my dear. You only say that because you've tamed him a bit. Every woman would rather tame a dragon than drive a sheep any day," Mary declared. "And you're no exception — and I don't blame you, considering what a very personable dragon he is. Really, when I saw you drive past with him in the car, I felt like the ranks of Tuscany and 'could scarce forbear to cheer.' "

"Idiot," laughed Jessica. "Though it was quite a moment," she agreed reflectively.

"I've asked my papa to find out all about him," Mary went on. "But, of course, men are so silly. They always find out the uninteresting things with the greatest ease, and forget to make the simplest enquiries about things that really matter. But, at least, I understand that the money is in shipping. His father started a private shipping line, and your Ford —"

"Not mine!" protested Jessica, but Mary ran on without paying attention to the interruption.

"Your Ford was made to start right at the bottom and work up, in the approved style."

"I approve of that style, too," Jessica said firmly.

"Oh, yes," Mary agreed indifferently. "Only one gets tired of the same story. All captains of industry start at the bottom and work up. I sometimes think it would be interesting to headline the story of a failure with, 'I started at the top and worked down,' don't you?"

Jessica laughed.

"Well, anyway, go on about Ford Onderley. What else did Mr. Skelton know about him?"

"Not very much," Mary admitted regretfully. "Only that he is head of the family firm now, and that there's a very tidy amount of money. He's not married or engaged."

"I know that," murmured Jessica. At which Mary put up her eyebrows and said:

"Darling, what an *interesting* conversation it must have been!"

"It was rather," Jessica admitted demurely, and they both laughed.

"Well, I'm going to get Father to arrange a nice little dinner party," Mary said reflectively. "After all, it's time we started being neighbourly. Just the Onderleys and yourself, and you might bring your nice Mrs. Forrest and David. And — let me see — we shall need another man. I suppose Arthur Tenby would do. He's quite sweet and ought to marry money. He's the sort of man who needs a rich wife to bring out the best in him."

"Who were you thinking of casting for the role of rich wife?" enquired Jessica interestedly.

"Why the Onderley sister, of course. There must be lots of money attached to her, as well as him."

"Ummm." Jessica shook her head. "I can't see her bringing out the best in an impecunious husband. *She's* the harder one of the two Onderleys, if you ask me."

"Very likely. Women often are harder than men," Mary said. "Anyway, it was only a passing idea. Arthur is always good as a fill-in, without my bothering about future advantages for him. I'll tell Father to get busy."

Jessica knew that Mary had only to issue affectionate orders for her father to carry them out. She was therefore not at all surprised to receive a definite for herself and the Forrests a couple of

invitation days later

something really pretty, won't you?" beg-
who liked her sister to look her best. And
d exaggeratedly when Jessica said regretfully:
isn't very much to choose from, pet. It
e to be my old pleated grey-green chiffon,
d."

dear! It's awfully pretty, of course, but not
tinguished," wailed Judy.

well, I don't know that *I'm* specially distinguished," Jessica said with a laugh.

"Yes, you are," cried Judy indignantly. "Mr. Forrest said you are. At least, he said you're awfully
unusual — like something beginning with 'd' that
means a wood nymph."

"I'm not a bit like a wood nymph," declared Jessica emphatically. But naturally she was gratified, and
she secretly wished very much that she had something
to wear at the dinner-party which would make her
look distinguished, as Judy put it.

However, the best she could do was to press her
old grey-green chiffon, and shampoo her copper-gold
hair the night before, and then brush it until it shone.

And when she had dressed her hair in its character-
istic little coronet on top of her head, and carefully
drawn in the waist of her dress to hide the fact that
it had been mended at least twice, she hoped she
would pass muster.

Judy surveyed the net result with qualified approval, and was just beginning her bit about something
distinguished being needed all over again when there
was a tap on the door and Mrs. Forrest came in.

"Do you mind doing me up the back, darling? It's
so difficult to manage for oneself with these 'poured-
in' effects," she explained.

And, while Jessica proceeded to fasten the simple
but perfect black frock, Judy said candidly:

"That's what I call distinguished."

"It's rather sweet, isn't it?" agreed Mrs. Forrest
with an air of contented understatement. And then,
because she was a genuinely kind-hearted woman, she

47

added, "Your sister's frock is very pretty t̶

"But not distinguished," objected Judy, c
the essential adjective.

"We-ell." Mrs. Forrest, now securely fasten
her own black model, surveyed Jessica critically. "
you need is something dramatic round your waist
and possibly at your neck as well. Something th
catches the eye without detracting from the very good
line of that dress, dear."

Jessica, well aware that her wardrobe contained
nothing which Mrs. Forrest could possibly consider
"dramatic," smiled and said:

"Yes, I dare say. But I really haven't got anything
like that."

"But *I* have," cried Mrs. Forrest, as sudden inspiration struck her. "I have the very thing, I do believe!"
And, before Jessica could form any polite protests,
she ran out of the room with the grace and speed
of a much younger woman.

She was not gone more than a few moments, and
Judy had hardly had time to say more than, "I hope
it's something *lovely*" before she came hurrying back
again.

In her hand she held a girdle of curious flat green
stones, set in a heavy, almost primitive gilt setting,
and from her rather dramatically outstretched fore-
finger dangled a short necklace of the same green
stones.

"Here you are, my dear. They were never my style
at all. Rather too primitive, you know. Curious rather
than chic."

And, as she spoke, she clasped the girdle round
Jessica's waist, and the thick, flat necklace round her
throat.

The effect was quite extraordinary. Even Jessica's
inexperienced eye told her that. While Judy bounced
up and down on the bed with satisfaction.

"You look lovely and fairy-tale-ish," she cried.
"And that funny shade of green makes your eyes
look greenish too, and your hair looks *marvellous,*
Jess!"

"The child's quite right," Mrs. Forrest declared.

"You look like a small edition of one of those Norse goddesses — one of the nicer ones, you know," she added, under the impression that mythology and Hans Andersen were one and the same thing.

But Jessica was in no mood to query the origin of the compliments being showered upon her. She knew, simply and deliciously, that she had never looked more attractive in her life. And, as she thanked Mrs. Forrest, her voice actually trembled with pleasure and excitement.

It was left to David to put the final and unmistakable seal of approval on her appearance. As he stood in the hall and watched her come down the stairs, he said, with an air of satisfaction:

"That's how I shall paint you. And it's going to be the best thing I've ever done."

So Jessica went off to Mary Skelton's party happily aware that she could reasonably hold her own with anyone else who was coming. And by "anyone else" she naturally meant Angela Onderley.

Jessica and the Forrests were the last to arrive, and the Onderleys and Arthur Tenby were already in the long, light, pleasant drawing-room, drinking their host's excellent sherry and engaging in the light, casual talk peculiar to people meeting each other for the first time.

As they came into the room, Jessica was aware that Ford Onderley turned to her (or perhaps it was to all three of them) with the natural pleasure of someone finding a familiar figure amid unfamiliar surroundings. And she was more than ever glad that Mrs. Forrest had lent her the belt and necklace to give "distinction" to her appearance.

Introductions followed, and Jessica found herself talking to Angela — a lovely, self-possessed, critical Angela who surveyed her, she thought, with not entirely friendly attention.

"I remember you now." Angela spoke politely rather than cordially. "You called to see my brother one evening, didn't you?"

"Yes," Jessica said. "I remember you too."

And she had the impression that Angela had no

idea of the reason for her visit, but would very much have liked to know it.

"Miss Skelton was just telling me about your deciding to keep a home going for your young brother and sister at The Mead. How enterprising of you," Angela said, but in rather the tone she would have used if commending a kitchen-maid's ambition to become a parlourmaid.

"Oh, I don't know that it's particularly enterprising." Jessica smiled with determined affability. "It's surprising what you find you can do, once an emergency arises."

And then she met Ford Onderley's eyes by chance, and his gaze was so quizzical and amused that she almost laughed in reply, and, glancing from Jessica to her brother, Angela must have noticed that they were sharing some private joke. At any rate, Jessica thought that her manner grew even colder, and she was glad when Angela turned away to talk to David.

During dinner the talk was fairly general, and it was not until afterwards that Ford Onderley had an opportunity to draw Jessica aside and enquire, with genuine interest:

"What are the latest reactions of Uncle Hector?"

"Oh, he's practically come to heel," Jessica explained. "Though he won't give a real decision until he and Aunt Miriam have had what they call 'a final discussion' when they come here next week on their way back from their holiday. But he's greatly impressed by your generosity — just as I am," she added with a quick, half-shy smile at him. "I know I didn't thank you properly the other evening, Mr. Onderley, but I've been thinking ever since how good you're being to us."

"All right, child." He smiled down at her. "Don't make too much of it."

"That," said Jessica gravely, "would be rather difficult. But there's one other thing —"

"Yes?"

"If Uncle Hector turns difficult again while he's here and seems hard to convince, would you — would you mind very much if I sent him down to see you?"

"Not at all. But do you think I should have a softening influence on him?"

"Oh, not *softening,* exactly," Jessica said, with an emphasis which he seemed to find amusing. "But he'll think that, if a stern business man like you is willing to support the venture, it can't be such a fantastic idea, after all."

"I see. Then I'll do my best."

"Thank you, Mr. Onderley. You're really very kind and understanding," Jessica said earnestly.

"Perhaps I'm trying to live down my dark reputation," he replied gravely, and Jessica laughed and flushed slightly.

Then she wished Angela had not chosen just that moment to glance in their direction. For the coldly speculative glance of those bright dark eyes seemed to attribute all sorts of disreputable motives for that very innocent laugh and blush.

"She doesn't like me," thought Jessica positively. And then: "Good heavens! she thinks I have designs on her brother."

The idea was so piquant and absurd that Jessica nearly laughed out loud, and she thought Angela could hardly be so intelligent as she looked if she could allow herself to be led astray on quite such a false trail. Anyway, possibly she herself was fanciful.

But that very evening she had unexpected confirmation of at least Angela's dislike of her and desire to disparage her. Goodbyes had been said and the Onderleys had already gone out to their car when Jessica picked up a scarf which Angela had dropped.

"Why, this is Miss Onderley's," she exclaimed. "I'll try to catch them." And she ran out into the darkened drive, where the Onderleys were already seated in their car, about to drive away.

As she came up from behind, they were still unaware of her presence when she was quite near, and, through the open window of the car, Angela's clear, cool tones floated distinctly to her.

"The Edom girl is quite pretty in a red-headed way, isn't she?" the casual voice said, and, though the wording might convey a contemptuous compliment, Angela was obviously implying to her brother that she thought Jessica Edom common and inconsiderable and not to be encouraged.

Jessica stopped dead, as though she had been struck in the face. So that, without any intention of eavesdropping, she heard Angela's brother reply coldly:

"No. 'Quite pretty' doesn't describe her in the least. She's lovely."

Then the car drove away, and Jessica was left standing, with the scarf forgotten in her hand. And, after a moment or two, she went back into the house, shaken, curiously enough, not so much by Angela's words as by her brother's.

"Didn't you catch them?" Mary glanced at the scarf. "I made sure you had. I thought I heard them drive away only a moment ago."

"I just didn't quite manage it," Jessica explained carefully. And Mary said:

"Well, it doesn't matter. I'm sure to see her passing the house during the next day or two."

On the way home, Jessica was rather quiet. But when Mrs. Forrest said, "It was a charming evening, wasn't it?" she agreed earnestly that indeed it had been.

During the next few days, Jessica was busy and saw nothing of any of her neighbours. But, on the day before Uncle Hector and Aunt Miriam were due to make their return visit, the twins begged that she would give herself a holiday and come with them on an expedition to a distant tarn, which was a favourite place for picnics, but too far and too dangerous a climb for the twins to go alone.

The Forrests were motoring over to Keswick for the day to see friends, so that the opportunity seemed a good one.

"And we don't know how often we shall have the chance again," Judy said with not unenjoyable melancholy. "If Uncle Hector does turn sticky, this'll be our last summer here."

"There's no need to anticipate Uncle Hector's turning sticky," Jessica assured her briskly. "But this certainly does seem to be a very special opportunity, so we'll go."

As soon as the Forrests had left, therefore, Jessica brought out a picnic basket, packed it with the speed and thoroughness of much experience, and, leaving a rather gratified Linda in charge, they set off on their long walk.

It was one of those cool, clear days, distinguished by a transient brightness which is all the more poignantly enjoyable because it may vanish at any moment.

"It'll rain before dark," Tom prophesied as they tramped up and up, over the turf and the heather, pausing at intervals to look back on the distant valley, or to measure the height at which they stood by comparison with one or other of the neighbouring hills.

"We shall be home before dark, though," Judy said. "Isn't it fun like this — just ourselves? Jessica, if you get married, Tom and I can stay on with you, can't we?"

"Of course," agreed Jessica, who was often called on to allay some remote anxiety roused by Judy's active imagination. "But I'm not thinking of getting married just now, anyway."

"No, but you never know when it *might* happen," said Judy, preparing for all eventualities. "I sometimes think Mr. Forrest might ask you."

"Judy! Don't be ridiculous. Whatever put such an idea into your head?"

"Well, he's going to paint your portrait, for one thing," Judy pointed out, a little shaken, however, by the emphasis of her sister's denial.

"That's nothing. He *is* a portrait-painter. He's probably going to paint Miss Onderley, come to that."

"Ah, but he's been asked to do that," said Judy shrewdly. "He did the asking himself where you were concerned."

"That doesn't mean a thing," Jessica explained hastily. "Except that he thinks I'm paintable, for some reason or other. It's probably my red hair. Some artists choose people they think look awful, just because they'll make an interesting study, you know."

"Oh," said Judy, who didn't seem to like this view of realism in art. "But I don't think Mr. Forrest chose you because he thinks you look awful," she added finally, as though having arrived at a satisfactory conclusion, and Jessica laughed.

"*I* think Mr. Onderley's more likely to ask you to marry him," Tom stated stolidly at this point.

"Good gracious! What extraordinary ideas you children have," cried Jessica. "I can't see the least reason why either of them should."

"Just because you're so nice," Judy said rather touchingly, while Tom said more judicially:

"I can. I'd marry you myself if I were grown-up and you weren't my sister. You know how to do everything well in a home, and you're not at all bad-looking, and you don't get cross about nothing, and you have a nice laugh."

"Well, really, I didn't know I was so highly appreciated in the home circle," declared Jessica, both amused and touched. "But I can't imagine that anyone will ever think so well of me as you two seem to, so, on the whole, perhaps I'd better stay with you and not get married at all."

The twins both seemed to find this a satisfactory solution, so the subject was abandoned in favour of the even more important one of the best time for lunch.

"I think the best way is to start eating as soon as you get hungry," Judy declared. "Then you get lots of energy for going on further."

"I don't. I think it's best to do all the hard climbing first. Then you can enjoy the eats and feel good," countered Tom.

Jessica — knowing from experience the value of the carrot-before-the donkey technique — firmly supported Tom's school of thought, and not until they reached the summit of the hill did she call a final halt, choose a spot sheltered from the sudden and capricious wind which had risen, and spread out the picnic supplies.

In front and far below lay the little tarn which was their ultimate goal, mirroring in its unruffled surface the clear blue of the sky overhead, so that it looked like an incredible, uncut jewel, carelessly thrown down at the foot of the surrounding hills.

"Isn't it a darling!" exclaimed Judy, regarding it with affectionate proprietorship. "I'm glad we waited until now to have lunch, because we can look at it all the time."

"We can look at it all the while we are climbing down to it, too," observed Tom practically. But Judy said that wasn't quite the same thing, because you had to look where you were going, as the path was rough.

"As a matter of fact" — Jessica glanced away a little doubtfully to the west — "I hate to say it, but I think we'd be wise not to go right down to the tarn this afternoon. It looks to me as though there's a heavy storm coming up soon."

"But we've got our macs," cried the twins in chorus. "We don't mind getting a bit wet."

"It's not that." Jessica looked faintly worried. "It's quite a stiff descent from here back home again, and if we spend the afternoon going to the tarn and back and it rains all the time, you know how greasy and difficult we shall find it coming down here again."

But the twins protested that it would be "all right," that it wouldn't rain for ages, that it was ridiculous to have come so far and not go down to the tarn. And, at the same time, out came the sun again, as though to prove Jessica overcautious, and she finally allowed herself to be overruled.

The picnic things were repacked and, with Tom swinging the now much lighter basket, they began the descent to the tarn.

They were halfway down when the rain began, but it only came in fitful gusts at first, and there were still rags of blue in a cloudy sky to seduce them into the hope that the rain would pass.

By the time they reached the tarn, however, it was coming down in sheets, and the once blue and placid little tarn looked dark and ruffled and menacing.

Not that this did not give it a certain sinister charm, and, in spite of the rain, they all three lingered for a short while in the partial shelter of some trees, responding with curious enjoyment to the wild, melancholy scene.

Then Jessica insisted that they must make their way back, particularly as it was obvious that the ever-thickening clouds would mean an unusually early nightfall.

Scrambling and slipping on the light, greasy mud of the path, they slowly began the ascent, while the rain poured down in that steady, pitiless way which characterises mountain districts. Even stout mackintoshes were hardly proof against it and, hot though they were from the upward struggle, they were also soaked and bedraggled by the time they reached the place where they had had their pleasant picnic.

As they finally came over the brow of the hill, and out of the shelter of the valley, a great capricious gust of wind struck them and almost took their breath away.

"Gosh, it's going to be fierce getting home from here," Tom said — but cheerfully, because stormy weather was no novelty to them.

· "It's downhill, so it won't be bad," Judy declared. But Jessica, while keeping her misgivings to herself, thought there were few things more unpleasant than a steep descent in wind and rain, down a slippery path with stones half-hidden in the mud.

At first the children made light of it, laughing a good deal at their attempts to keep their balance. But after a while the adventure began to assume more the character of a struggle than a joke, and they became more silent.

The rain seemed to come at them from every direction at once, and the wind rose and fell with a capricious violence that forced them at one moment to press against it as though it were a concrete thing, and, the next, to stagger at the sudden withdrawal of the opposition.

"Have my hand, Judy," said Jessica, suspecting that her little sister was beginning to feel scared.

But Judy was anxious to demonstrate her independence, and she firmly shook her head and slithered on ahead, trying to keep up as good a show as Tom.

There was one point where the path took a sharp curve, narrowed and overhung a bank so steep that it might almost be considered a precipice, and it was here that Jessica felt her heart come into her throat as she saw Judy slither, unaided but determined, in the wake of Tom.

"Judy!" Anxiety sharpened her voice. "Keep further in, dear. Wait for me and I'll give you a hand."

"I don't *want* a hand," cried Judy, defiant with weariness and fright. And she glanced back crossly at Jessica, at the same time as she took an uncertain step forward.

In one second the child's feet shot from under her.

Jessica saw her clutch at nothing, heard her cry out, and, the next moment — like something seen in a nightmare — Judy disappeared over the edge of the cliff.

CHAPTER FOUR

JESSICA never quite forgot the horror of that moment when Judy's red beret vanished from sight.

She called wildly to Tom, who was tramping on ahead, unaware of the disaster behind him. And then, clinging to a wind-bent but stout little tree at the edge of the cliff, she leaned over as far as she could and looked down, dreading to think what she might see there.

As Tom panted up behind her, demanding, "What's hap-happened? Where's Judy?" she made out her little sister, lying on a wide ledge, not really very far down the side of the cliff — but lying quite still.

"Stay where you are," she ordered Tom. "I'm going down."

And, because he was a sensible child who had been taught to obey, he just gave one gasp and said:

"All right. But it's not so steep further along the path. Try that, and then work your way back once you get further down."

Jessica saw the advice was good, and ran further down the path at a pace she would not have thought possible three minutes ago. Then, holding fast to bushes and shrubs, she lowered herself over the side of the cliff, and began the descent to the ledge where Judy lay.

Once her foot slipped — and found nothing. And she hung by her hands for several throbbing seconds, while she felt desperately for a foothold where none seemed to be. Then her foot found some sort of resting place and, venturing her weight on it by frightened degrees, she found that it held, so that she was able to take the strain at last from her aching, trembling arms.

And, all the while, silhouetted against the darkening sky, she could see the sturdy, comforting outline of Tom, faithfully standing guard — from which she derived an inordinate amount of courage and consolation.

It seemed a long while — but in reality it could have been only a few minutes — before she reached the ledge, which proved to be narrower than it had looked from above, and with a sickening slope outwards towards further depths. Only the fact that she had caught against a tree stump had prevented Judy from rolling further.

As Jessica bent over the child, Judy gave a faint whimper and began to show signs of returning consciousness. Divided between unnerving joy at finding her alive and fear that too much movement might precipitate them both further, Jessica took the little girl in her arms, and said over and over again:

"You're all right, darling. Don't be frightened. You're all right."

After a few moments, Judy returned to full consciousness with a start which brought Jessica's heart into her mouth.

"Careful, Judy. We've got to keep rather still for the moment," she explained quickly, while she tried to imagine how on earth she was to get a frightened, and possibly injured child up a cliff which had been difficult enough to come down.

At that moment, even Tom's stoicism showed signs of cracking, and he shouted down anxiously:

"Is she all right, Jess?"

Jessica looked up at his good, devoted little figure, peering over at them both.

"Yes, she's alive and I think she's all right," she called back encouragingly.

But Judy gave a sob and whispered dolefully.

"I'm not all right. My leg's twisted under me and I can't move it."

"I'll raise you, darling, and then you see what you can do," Jessica said, and moved her cautiously.

But, at the first real movement, Judy screamed and so obviously turned faint again, that Jessica realised, with a sinking heart, that it was real injury, rather than fright and shock, that had rendered the child helpless.

Fortunately, she was used to making her own decisions — even hard ones — in a crisis, and she accepted the fact that, unaided, she could not possibly move Judy from the ledge. Equally, she could not leave the child there, frightened and soaked and with night coming on fast. That left only Tom on whom to rely and — not for the first time in her life — she thanked heaven that he was such a reliable child.

"Tom," she called, "listen to me carefully."

"Yes?" came back the answer, and, though anxiety had unsteadied his voice and even, she thought from the quaver, produced a few tears, she knew that he would do what she told him.

"Judy's hurt her leg and I can't get her up alone, so I'll have to stay with her. Leave all the baskets and things on the path, dear, and go down to the village as fast as you can. Don't take any risks, Tom — but go as fast as you can with safety. Go to Mr. Skelton, and fetch the doctor too, if you can. But, anyway, tell them they'll need ropes to bring up someone who's injured."

"Yes. It's all right. I know what to tell them." Tom sounded more like himself again. "Is — is she much hurt, Jess?"

"I'm all right," piped Judy rather weakly. And Jessica reinforced that with a confidence she was far from feeling:

"She's not dangerously hurt. But the sooner we get her home and to bed, the better. Now, off you go."

"I shan't be long," cried Tom confidently. And his figure disappeared.

There was a short silence after he had gone, and then Judy said, with rather patent anxiety:

"How long do you think he *will* be, Jess?"

"Oh, not very long." Jessica sounded as though the whole experience were nothing very sensational. "He walks very fast, you know, and he may meet someone long before he gets to the village. Someone on a bicycle or in a car."

"He won't do that till he gets to the main road," objected Judy.

"No. But he'll soon be there," Jessica insisted with more heartiness than she felt, particularly when she reflected how unlikely it was that any cyclist or motorist would be out on this stormy night for any reason but extreme necessity.

Judy, however, seemed satisfied with her optimistic forecasts, because she sank into docile silence once more.

For a few moments, Jessica was thankful for the fact. Then she realised that the child was cold and over-quiet, and she guessed distractedly that she was beginning to suffer the after-affects of shock.

And still the rain poured down relentlessly.

In spite of Judy's protests, Jessica managed to move them both into the tiny bit of shelter which the cliff afforded, and then, taking off her own raincoat, she put it round both of them, bundling Judy up close against her and trying to keep her warm.

It was too dark now to see the time by her watch, and, in any case, she had forgotten to look at the time when Tom had gone. She could only guess at the distance he might have covered, and the consequent length of time which they still had to wait before help might come.

Meanwhile, all she could do was try not to shiver too violently under the onslaught of wind and rain, and try to reassure Judy from time to time that she was quite warm without her raincoat and that help would soon come.

After a while, Judy drifted off into something between uneasy sleep and semi-consciousness. And presently Jessica too seemed at any rate to lose much consciousness of the passage of time. She was only aware of a deadly ever-present sense of anxiety, and a degree of physical discomfort beyond anything she had ever imagined.

"But at least I'm not cold any more," she muttered to herself once. And then she wondered if the burning, unnatural heat which seemed to oppress her were not even more unbearable than the cruel cold. Her weary, numbed brain was still struggling with this question — which seemed to have assumed a ridiculous degree of importance — when she was aware of a voice overhead, calling her name, and some inexplicable, blinding light blazed with what seemed unnecessary cruelty into her dazzled eyes as she looked up.

"Jessica —" and, incredibly, it was Ford Onderley's voice which recalled her to full consciousness. "Jessica, answer me! Are you still down there." And she realised that the light came from a powerful torch, with which he was raking the side of the cliff.

"Yes, we're down here," she called hoarsely. And then, most unreasonably, "Put out that light."

At least it was withdrawn from her immediate vicinity, and, since she didn't hear his voice any more, she became overwhelmed by the dreadful thought that she had offended him and he had gone away.

This seemed not at all unreasonable to her in her fevered, half delirious state, and the magnitude of the disaster made her cry at last.

"Please don't go away," she sobbed. "I'm sorry I was rude. Oh, please don't go away."

And then his voice, almost beside her, said:

"Don't be a silly child. Of course, I'm not going away. Here, drink some of this, and let me have a look at the little girl."

Jessica found herself drinking scalding hot coffee from the cup of a thermos flask. And then her head was much clearer, although it still ached a great deal, and she was vaguely aware that she had been behaving in a strangely foolish way, but she thought she would be all right now.

He had gently taken Judy's weight from her aching arms and, by the light of the torch which she now saw was suspended round his neck, he made a cursory examination of the unconscious child.

"How did you get here?" whispered Jessica hoarsely.

"I came ahead of the others because my car is faster," he explained briefly. "They'll be here in a few minutes, with a sling to get Judy up to the top. Here, take my coat. Have you been sitting here *without* a coat?"

"I put my raincoat round both of us, but it only covered part of me. Anyway, I'm not cold — I'm hot," Jessica explained, and then began to shiver so violently that her teeth rattled in her head.

Without any more argument, he slipped out of his heavy coat — momentarily she wondered how he had come so quickly down the cliff in it — and wrapped it round her. And, at the same time, voices and more lights overhead announced the arrival of the rest of the rescue party.

Jessica was always very vague afterwards about the details of how she and Judy were hauled up the cliff side, and hurried down to the waiting ambulance in the main road far below. Judy, of course, was carried on a stretcher, and she thought that Ford Onderley half carried her most of the way. On the final stretch of the path he must have carried her, because she had no recollection whatever of walking it.

Then she was bundled into his car and driven home at what seemed like nightmare speed, while he assured her that Judy would be taken straight to hospital and well cared for.

"She'd rather come home," sobbed Jessica, overcome by inexplicable tears. "Why don't they bring her home and let me nurse her?"

"You won't be in any condition to nurse anyone for a while," Ford Onderley told her firmly.

This seemed a monstrous imposition to the half-delirious Jessica — that Ford Onderley should stand between her and Judy. And she said, with the conviction that the fact had been proved to her:

"You're a very hard man."

"Possibly," he agreed equably. "And you're a very sick girl, at the moment, my dear. So stop arguing, like a good child, and let someone else make the decisions just now."

She wanted to say that *he* had no right to make them, but the argument suddenly seemed pointless and quite unbearably difficult to continue, so she lapsed into silence, though she was aware that she muttered rather unintelligibly from time to time.

After that, she was not aware of anything much, until she found she was in bed — which was an exquisite relief, only it didn't appear to do much for the alternate shivering and burning which seemed to have returned with redoubled force, and still less for the inexplicable pains which were now in every limb.

Jessica had the queer impression that days and nights ran into each other, without much real regard for time. And sometimes Mrs. Forrest was there, and sometimes Aunt Miriam, and — most often of all — a complete stranger in a nurse's uniform.

She knew, with a detached, impersonal awareness, that she was very ill, and at times she even remembered about the children and was worried. But she felt too physically weak to do anything about any problem, and an occasional muttered, "Is Judy all right?" was all that she could achieve.

It was a soft, bright afternoon when at last she came to full consciousness again, and for a long while she lay there, just quietly enjoying the pale sunshine which shone in through the window opposite, and the first faint stirrings of returning health. She felt ridiculously and unutterably weak, but at least the pain was gone, and her skin felt cool and normal.

For the first time, she was able to think back coherently to that scene on the cliff side, and to wonder with quickening anxiety what had happened to Judy and Tom — and herself.

She wished fretfully that someone would come and tell her what she wanted to know. And then, as though in answer to her thought, there was a sound of the door opening and voices talking quietly.

First came the voice which Jessica found she associated with the nurse, and it said:

"Well, you can just peep at her. But I doubt if she will know you."

And then Mary — dear, thrice-welcome Mary! — replied, in an unusually subdued tone:

"I won't disturb her. I'll just look at her."

"Oh, Mary darling, is that you?" Jessica spoke with more energy than she would have thought possible a moment ago. "Come in and talk to me!"

There were pleased exclamations, and both the nurse and Mary — carrying pink roses and looking surprisingly as though she had tears in her eyes — came within Jessica's range of vision.

"*That's* better!" declared the nurse with brisk cheerfulness, while Mary just bent down and kissed her, as though she found it rather difficult to say anything.

"Only ten minutes," warned the nurse. But Jessica held Mary's hand tightly and said:

"Sit down and tell me about everything. How is Judy?"

"Getting on splendidly. The poor poppet had broken her leg, you know, and got a nasty knock on the head too, but she's making an excellent recovery now." Mary drew up a chair, and obviously meant to make the most of the ten minutes allowed her. "You must have kept her very well protected, Jess, for she hardly suffered from exposure at all," she added, looking very kindly down at her friend.

"I was terrified for her," Jessica owned, "and I'm so relieved she's getting on now. And Tom? My good reliable little Tom!"

Mary smiled.

"He didn't suffer from anything worse than a bad cold. I had him home with me, and kept him in bed for the first week."

"The first — week?" Jessica repeated curiously. "How long is it since it happened then?"

"Three weeks — going on for four," Mary said, and an unwonted shade of anxiety crossed her face again.

"Nearly four *weeks?*" Jessica looked astonished. "I can't believe it! What on earth has been the matter with me, then?"

There was the slightest hesitation, and then, because Mary knew her friend too well to suppose she would accept prevarication, she said as lightly as she could:

"You've indulged in a nasty little bout of rheumatic fever, darling, and a nice fright you've given us all."

"Rheumatic fever! No wonder I feel so weak," Jessica exclaimed.

"Um-hm. It's pretty weakening," Mary agreed.

"It's a bit apt to leave one with a funny heart, too, isn't it?" Jessica said, rather carefully avoiding Mary's glance.

"O-oh" — Mary seemed just as anxious to avoid Jessica's eyes, for some reason — "not if one's careful. You don't need to start worrying about yourself, darling. You're getting on splendidly now."

"I'm not worrying about myself," Jessica explained slowly. "At least, not in the usual way, I mean. It's only — so much depends on my being well and strong during the next year, Mary."

"Yes, I know, pet. But these things usually smooth themselves out. The great thing is not to worry, because that will only put back your full recovery."

"I know," Jessica agreed, with a sigh. "I'll try not to worry." Then, after a moment, she added: "Who's running the house, Mary?"

"Your Aunt Miriam is."

"Aunt Miriam! I say, that is good of her," exclaimed Jessica, with a stab of genuine contrition for the little she had appreciated Aunt Miriam up to now.

"Yes, I suppose it is." Mary's praise was more qualified. "But there isn't very much to harass her, you know. Judy's still in hospital, of course, and Tom is with me. So all Aunt Miriam has to do is run around after Linda and the nurse, and see they don't sit down too often. She's good at it," Mary added reflectively.

"Did Uncle Hector decide on a trained nurse when he arrived, the day after the accident?" Jessica enquired, trying to visualise the scene and failing.

"No," Mary said, a little dryly. "Ford Onderley decided on a trained nurse, long before Uncle Hector put in an appearance."

"Ford Onderley did!"

"Um-hm. I can tell you, he looked around and gave orders as though The Mead belonged to him."

"Well, it does," Jessica reminded Mary mildly.

"Yes, of course, in a way. But I think the Forrests felt he threw his weight about a bit too much — taking charge of everything, including you."

"What do you mean? — including me."

"Well, he just carried you in, I understand, and right up to your bedroom, issuing his orders for doctors and nurses and peaches and brandy as he went, so to speak," explained Mary, grinning rather teasingly.

"Don't be absurd." Jessica laughed weakly.

"Anyway, he then proceeded to carry out all his own orders. I will say that for him," Mary conceded. "He phoned the doctor, and secured a nurse, on his own initiative, and then fetched peaches and brandy, or whatever it was, in unlimited supplies from Oaklands. I believe there's been a sort of pipeline of luxury supplies from Oaklands here, ever since," Mary added thoughtfully.

"Mary, how very kind of him! But he shouldn't," Jessica protested a little worriedly. "And it was frightfully nice of him to get a trained nurse, but she's an expensive luxury, and he ought to have consulted Uncle Hector first. I'm sure he would have said Aunt Miriam preferred to look after me herself or something."

"I think that's just what Uncle Hector did say," Mary agreed.

"What do you mean?" Jessica glanced at her quickly.

"Well" — Mary bit her lip and laughed — "I'm not really supposed to tell you anything but sweet and soothing news, but I believe there were a few sharp words between Uncle Hector and the dictator of Oaklands, and Ford Onderley said *he* was underwriting the expenses of your illness, so Uncle Hector needn't bother."

"Mary, he didn't! What impertinence!"

"Nice, convenient impertinence," Mary pointed out reflectively.

"But I couldn't have him doing such a thing. I haven't known the man more than a few weeks. And during most of those I've been unconscious," Jessica added with an irrepressible gleam of humour.

"Well, my pet, don't worry about that either for the moment," Mary advised her. "Just you get well, and then you can sort everything out for yourself — and you may find that I've got this story a bit wrong."

"I shouldn't be surprised," Jessica agreed. "How did you hear all this, anyway? Or have you just invented it?"

"Really, Jess! From my best friend!" Mary laughed.

"As a matter of fact, Mrs. Forrest gave me a rather lively account of what happened during the first few days."

"Oh, the Forrests!" Jessica suddenly remembered their position in the scheme of things. "What on earth has happened to them during all this?"

"Well, they stayed on for the first few days, and then Mrs. Forrest said, very reasonably, that they were probably more in the way than of assistance, with illness in the house," Mary explained. "So they went to an hotel at Keswick. They had friends there, hadn't they?" Jessica nodded. "I think they're returning to London shortly, but no doubt they will come over to see you before they finally go."

"Yes. I expect so."

Jessica suddenly felt inordinately tired again, and a good deal depressed. Where were all her nice plans now? Her ideal paying guests, who were to have made such a good beginning for her, had not been able to stay. And the flimsy foundations of her hopes were now exposed. Two or three weeks of illness — and a frighteningly weakening and disabling illness, at that — had been sufficient to put back, if not to destroy, all her hopeful planning.

Mary evidently saw the change in expression, because she said quickly:

"I expect we've talked long enough. I'll have that nurse calling out for my blood if I don't go soon, because I expect you tire rather easily just yet, dear."

Jessica nodded.

"It's not just being tired," she said rather sadly. "I can't help — worrying a bit, too."

"Oh, you mustn't do that," Mary exclaimed. "It's the very last thing you should do! In fact, I had very strict instructions to see that you didn't."

"From whom?" Jessica smiled faintly.

"Your Ford Onderley, as a matter of fact."

"Mary! He's not 'my' Ford Onderley. And, anyway, what has he got to do with it?"

"In my view, rather little," Mary admitted. "In his, quite a lot, I believe. I met him on my way here, and he stopped me and asked after you. When he heard I hoped to see you, he said I was to tell you most emphatically not to worry about anything. In fact, I'm afraid he added that he would see everything was all right, which I thought rather officious of him."

"Oh, Mary" — Jessica gave a doubtful little laugh and bit her lip — "I don't know what to say about him. It *is* officious of him, in a way, of course, and I'm afraid he has a fixed belief that he's entitled to interfere when and where he pleases. But he does mean it kindly, I'm sure. He may just have wanted me to know that I — that I needn't worry about the rent and —"

"Good heavens! I should hope you *needn't* worry about the rent in the middle of a bad illness," interrupted Mary indignantly.

"No, no — I didn't mean it that way. He made a wonderfully generous arrangement about the rent, so that I could start my paying-guest idea. Now, perhaps he's thinking the same as I am, that — that it may not be possible to carry out the idea." Jessica's voice trembled slightly with distress and disappointment, in spite of herself, but she recovered her composure and added quickly. "At least, it may not be possible for some time. I dare say he was trying to convey the fact that, even in the changed circumstances, I needn't worry."

"Possibly." Mary looked amusedly sceptical. "Personally, I thought he was trying to convey the fact that as a despotic, if benevolent, landlord, he felt a personal responsibility for you, Judy, Tom and The Mead, generally."

Jessica laughed faintly and said, "I don't know which is more absurd — you or he."

But, long after Mary had gone — driven out by a menacingly bright but very determined nurse — Jessica lay there and thought about Ford Onderley and his apparent determination to take a hand in her affairs.

Well, Mary was right when she said that worrying would only retard her recovery, so she would try not to worry. And, curiously enough, in her endeavours to regard the future philosophically, Jessica found that she rested, with illogical relief, on the thought that Ford Onderley *was* there.

After that, there were no more periods of wandering. Jessica found that she was aware — indeed, very sharply aware — of most things which were going on around her now. Not only the informative visits of Aunt Miriam and the uninformative comments of the nurse, but the familiar sounds from other parts of the house. Sounds for which she could either unhesitatingly supply the source, from old experience, or worry about because they indicated a new order of things with which it was going to be very difficult to cope.

It was odd and disturbing, for instance, to hear Uncle Hector clearing his throat portentously — which he frequently did — and to reflect that there he was in the house, the living embodiment of opposition to the kind of life she and the twins had hoped to have. But, think as she would, she could not formulate any useful arguments against his known views, and it was no good tiring herself in the attempt to do so just now.

One afternoon Tom came to see her, and, if he displayed some degree of homesickness in the first shock of seeing her, it was perfectly obvious that he was extremely happy at the Skeltons' house.

"I say, you *have* been proved right about that walk, haven't you?" said Tom, who was a literal-minded child and liked the odd ends of conversations and circumstances tied up neatly.

"Have I?" Jessica smiled at him. "What walk do you mean?"

"Oh, Jess!" He seemed astonished by her lack of comprehension. "Don't you remember? You kept on saying it was silly of us to go right down to the tarn that afternoon, as we'd have difficulty getting back if it rained. And, my goodness, were you right!"

Jessica laughed.

"I'll say I was," she agreed. "But never mind now. I think that little burst of sunshine after lunch deceived us all. How is Judy?"

"You are nice, the way you never nag and say, 'I

told you so,' " remarked Tom, taking first things first. "Judy's fine now. They let me go to see her every day at the hospital, and they're very jolly there and let me do one or two jobs. But they won't let me go in and see an operation, and I think it's rather mean of them, don't you? Because I'll never have such an opportunity again, and it's all knowledge, isn't it?"

"I dare say it's knowledge you can do without for the moment," his sister told him firmly. "And stop being a gruesome child. Is Judy happy there?"

"Yes, very. Oh, she gave me a note for you." And Tom extracted from his pocket an envelope which showed some signs of wear and tear.

It was written in pencil, in Judy's very round hand-writing, and informed Jessica — with a certain degree of originality in the spelling — that she was very well and would soon be "hopping about with a crutch."

"Poor old Jess! You had the worst time in the end, I think," Judy's letter went on. *"But Mary says you are better now. Mr. Onderley comes to see me on visiting days and brings lovely things. Has he been to see you yet? If not, wear that nice blue frilly dressing-jacket when he comes. The one Mary gave you for Christmas that looks like a film star.*

"Lots of love from

"Judy."

Jessica slowly folded up the note again and smiled. "She sounds quite happy."

"Oh, yes," Tom stated confidently. "She is."

"It's very kind of Mr. Onderley to go and see her." Jessica bit her lip thoughtfully. "I'm glad he likes her."

"I think," Tom said, with a sort of naïve shrewd-ness, "it's because he likes you."

Jessica murmured, "Oh, nonsense." But, after her young brother had gone — just as after Mary's de-parture — the person with whom her thoughts were mostly concerned was Ford Onderley.

Why was he being so specially kind to them all? Was it sheer good nature? Or a humorously perverse desire to show that he was not the hard landlord he was supposed to be? Or did he, for some reason she could not fathom, consider that she and the twins were in some way his concern?

It was more than Jessica could decide — particularly as she felt too weak to tackle anything really problematical just now.

However, it seemed that she was not the only one who thought Ford Onderley's continued attentions required some explanation. Aunt Miriam, who belonged to what is usually referred to as "the old-fashioned school" (meaning that she had some regard for appearances and the conventions), came in the next afternoon with a large basket of fruit and a rather perplexed expression.

"Mr. Onderley called with this for you, Jessica," she said. "He really does seem very *attentive,* my dear."

"Yes. He's very kind," murmured Jessica, feeling faintly self-conscious — and angry with herself for being so.

"Jessica, just how well do you and Mr. Onderley know each other?" Aunt Miriam pushed up her spectacles on to her forehead and regarded her niece rather severely. "Your uncle and I supposed he had known your father for a long time, and you children most of your lives. But, since he is obviously quite a young man, that isn't possible. *Did* your father know him well?"

"No," Jessica said, in a rather small voice. "He didn't know him at all."

"Jessica! Really, my dear, when you went to see him about the new agreement, did you know him at all well?"

"No, Aunt Miriam. It was the first time I had met him," Jessica confessed.

"You should have told your uncle, and let him go. It would have been *much* better."

"But I got what we all wanted," Jessica pointed out, not without satisfaction, because she very much doubted if Uncle Hector would have done as much.

"That isn't the only point," Aunt Miriam said, and she meant it. "There are such things as decent appearances."

"Really, Aunt Miriam, I don't think I've outraged those," Jessica protested a little dryly.

"Well, my dear, I don't think *he* has sufficient regard for them," Aunt Miriam retorted. "He actually spoke to your uncle about — about paying the costs of your illness."

"That was absurd, of course," Jessica agreed quickly.

"And now he talks of intending to be your first visitor when you are up."

"*Does* he?"

"And there are all these expensive presents. In my young days, that would have been called making a girl conspicuous." Aunt Miriam pressed her lips together disapprovingly. "To my way of thinking, there are only two people towards whom a man can act as Mr. Onderley is acting."

"Really, Aunt Miriam?" Jessica said curiously. "And who are they?"

"Either an old family friend — and it seems you certainly are not that."

"Or else —?" pressed Jessica, half-amused and half-annoyed.

"Or else a fiancée, Jessica," her aunt stated firmly.

CHAPTER FIVE

AT AUNT Miriam's preposterous suggestion, Jessica opened her eyes wide and laughed.

"Oh, Aunt Miriam dear, there's absolutely nothing like that! Really, you must believe me. I don't even know him very well."

"Then he shouldn't be acting the way he is," Aunt Miriam retorted. And Jessica had a momentary and quite dreadful fear that Uncle Hector would be instructed to ask Ford Onderley his "intentions" next time he called at the house.

"It's really only that he is a very generous man — with a rather unconventional way of showing it, if you like," Jessica explained earnestly. "And I assure you, Aunt Miriam, I'll put the matter right in a tactful way the first moment I see him. I think I agree that he had better be my first visitor," she added reflectively. "It seems that a few early explanations would be in order. How soon can I have visitors, do you think?"

"You won't be out of bed for another week or ten days," her aunt informed her, and Jessica accepted the obvious implication that Aunt Miriam would not countenance male visitors while her niece was still in bed.

But Aunt Miriam was amiably defeated on this minor point, for two or three days later the Forrests called, and David, as well as his mother, was swept upstairs on the tidal wave of Evelyn Forrest's sympathetic enquiries, comments, exclamations and suggestions.

"You poor child!" she cried, kissing Jessica with real anxiety and kindness. "What a terrible time you must have had."

"Well, I'm better now," Jessica explained with a smile, and gave her free hand to David, who held it longer than was necessary, and just looked his sympathy while his mother's stream of eloquence ran on.

"It seems you were quite a heroine," Mrs. Forrest

said admiringly. "Protecting Judy all that time, at the expense of your own safety. It *does* seem hard that your only reward should be to have all your future plans spoilt. But I dare say everything will work out all right and that your aunt and uncle will arrange something to please you all." And she looked very significantly at Aunt Miriam, as though willing her to act in what she, herself, considered the right manner.

Aunt Miriam, however, merely looked stiff and remote, as though she considered Mrs. Forrest was presuming. Which, of course, she was.

Jessica glanced sharply from one to the other.

"What makes you think all my future plans will be spoilt, Mrs. Forrest?" she asked, with deceptive quietness.

"Well, darling, you'll have to go very slow for a while with that poor little heart of yours, and —"

"Mother, don't you think we're talking rather too much?" interrupted David, who had not been able to talk at all up till now. But Jessica broke in quickly:

"Do finish what you were going to say, Mrs. Forrest. About my having to go slow and —? What else were you going to say?"

"Only that you certainly won't be able to run this place and take paying guests, dear, for *quite* a long time." Then, as she saw Jessica bite her lip and turn even paler, she cried anxiously and belatedly: "Oh, I do hope I'm not giving away any secrets?"

"You're speaking a little out of turn," her son told her dryly, with something as near to anger as his good nature allowed.

"Oh, no," Jessica said softly. "Oh, no. It doesn't matter really. No one had told me — yet, in so many words, but I knew it pretty well, just from putting two and two together."

"It was just common sense," commented Aunt Miriam a little repressively. And Jessica could not help feeling that some very unpalatable arrangements were going to be made in the name of common sense.

"Let's talk about something else," she said quickly. "Tell me what you've been doing. I'm afraid my little escapade rather spoilt your holiday, didn't it?"

"Oh, we've managed very well," David assured her. "Don't you worry about us. We made ourselves quite comfortable at our hotel and, though we'll soon be going back to London for a while, Mother is talking of taking a furnished house near here for the autumn."

"I simply *must* be here to see the autumn colours," declared Mrs. Forrest rather emotionally. "It must be the most beautiful sight."

"It will probably rain a great deal at that time of year," remarked Aunt Miriam, to whom dry feet were more important than autumn colours.

"Very possibly. We shall see some beautiful rain and cloud effects as well, then," retorted Mrs. Forrest, determined to show that she had a soul above mundane matters.

"It will be lovely to have you for neighbours," Jessica said tactfully, "if — if we're still here."

"Of course you must still be here," David declared. "That's half the attraction of the place for us. And, anyway, when else am I going to get that portrait of you done?"

Jessica smiled at him.

"Oh, yes — the portrait. It seems I've held up the course of artistic inspiration as well as your holiday. I feel very guilty."

"You needn't, dear," Mrs. Forrest assured her before David could answer for himself. "He has been getting on with his portrait of Mr. Onderley's sister instead."

"Have you really?" Jessica turned back to David with interest. "Then you did decide to paint her, after all?'

"Yes. She's a most interesting subject. Much more so than I expected," David said candidly. "Though why I came to any decision about her before I saw her, I don't know. It's always silly to do that."

"Oh, well, you didn't like her brother, dear," his mother explained equably, "and you thought she would be the same type. Personally, of course, I think she is. I dislike cold and arrogant people, don't you?" she added, appealing to Aunt Miriam, as though there could reasonably be two opinions about this.

"Certainly I dislike them," said Aunt Miriam, surprised to find herself in agreement with Mrs. Forrest, even on such an unexceptionable generality as this.

"I don't think Mr. Onderley is cold and arrogant," Jessica stated firmly, more interested in the particular than the general.

"Well, you wouldn't call him warm and humble, dear," protested Mrs. Forrest.

"No — not *humble*." Jessica laughed at the word in connection with Ford Onderley. "But I think he's essentially generous and warm-hearted. And, if he is a little bit arrogant, it's more a mannerism than — I mean —"

Jessica caught Aunt Miriam's eyes upon her with such an extremely speculative and disapproving light in them that, to her intense annoyance, she suddenly found herself blushing and stammering.

"Well, anyway, he has been very kind to me," she finished hastily and a little crossly.

"You're rather an easy person to be kind to, Jessica," David told her with a very charming smile, and the awkward moment was neatly glossed over.

After that, he seemed to take charge of the conversation, and Jessica realised, with something like relief, that she could lie back and smile and listen, and contribute only an occasional word or two. David, she thought affectionately, was like that. He was a born smoother of difficulties, and could be trusted to size up a situation and deal with it, without having to have it explained to him in words of one syllable.

He knew she was just a little tired, and wanted to be amused and soothed and not to have controversial topics raked over.

"David is all that one means by a really nice man," thought Jessica lazily. "Dear and kind and easy to live with."

In this Mrs. Forrest would have entirely agreed with her — and probably have pointed out that it was largely due to her own admirable training.

Even Aunt Miriam, who was a difficult person to please, could find nothing in David of which to disapprove. Indeed, when the Forrests had gone — after promising to come at least once more before their departure to London — she observed that he was "a very steady and likeable young man, which was surprising in an artist."

"Yes, he's a darling," Jessica agreed.

"I don't wish to sound censorious," continued Aunt Miriam, who did not in the least mind sounding censorious, "but I should say that she is both flighty and interfering. Rather absurd in a woman of her age."

"She's very kind," Jessica insisted, "and, if she is a little — flighty, as you say, she also has plenty of common sense and would be a good friend in an emergency."

"Possibly." Aunt Miriam sounded as though she thought the possibility remote. "But he is the really stable one of the two. He will make an excellent husband for some lucky girl. That is, if his mother ever lets him get away," she added, with a certain grim shrewdness.

"Oh, Aunt Miriam! I don't think she's a very possessive parent. Do you?"

"Not outwardly. She is too clever for that," was Aunt Miriam's expressed opinion. "But I don't doubt she has seen to it on several occasions that either he has been moved on at the right moment, or some girl has been moved off."

This was so nearly epigrammatic for Aunt Miriam that Jessica laughed aloud.

"Perhaps it's just that he can look after himself, in spite of his charm and good nature," she suggested. "But I agree with you that he can't have reached his age without several girls having had a more or less decorous try at making him give up bachelordom."

"Of course. It's in the nature of things, with a really nice man," stated Aunt Miriam with austere realism.

"I'm glad you like him." Jessica smiled, thinking it was just as well that Aunt Miriam should approve of *one* of her men friends.

"Yes," her aunt said reflectively. "Though there is no real facial likeness, he reminds me of your dear uncle when he was younger."

Jessica was struck dumb with astonishment at the disclosure of this curious parallel. Personally, she could find no single point of resemblance between her ponderous, worthy uncle and the gay and charming David, and she could only wonder silently at the miracles which can be wrought by a personal point of view.

She was also faintly touched at the thought that someone could actually look at Uncle Hector with the eye of romance. Undoubtedly, Aunt Miriam had married him in the belief that he would make an excellent husband — and he had not let her down. Therefore she could pay no young man a higher compliment than to think that she detected in him the same lasting qualities which had distinguished her own husband.

"It's really rather a nice comment on Uncle Hector," thought Jessica, amused and touched. "Oh dear, if only he had included a certain capacity for taking generous risks, along with all his other virtues!"

But that brought her back so closely to her own problems that she sighed and said abruptly:

"Aunt Miriam, how long am I going to be laid by the heels here?"

"Do you mean — when will you be up?"

"No. I meant — when will I be able to live a normal, energetic life again?" Jessica said.

"Not for some months, my dear." Aunt Miriam spoke kindly, but quite finally. "We didn't mean to discuss the question with you so early in your convalescence, but" — she pressed her lips together disapprovingly — "Mrs. Forrest has rather precipitated matters. I'm afraid there isn't any question of your keeping this place running as a separate home, as you hoped. The children will have to go to boarding school, as soon as Judy is sufficiently well, and I hope you will manage to make yourself happy with your uncle and me until you are strong enough to earn your own living."

In spite of being keenly sensible of the fact that her aunt and uncle were being very generous, Jessica was too weak to keep back the tears of disappointment that came into her eyes.

"Oh, Aunt Miriam, *please* don't let's decide this

in a hurry. Practically speaking, Mr. Onderley was willing to let us stay here rent free for a year until —"

"Jessica, you must see how impossible and unsuitable that would be!" exclaimed Aunt Miriam sharply. "It was a considerable concession that he was willing to take the year's rent in arrear. It would be nothing less than dishonest to accept that condition, knowing that, for most of the year at least, you would be unable to do anything towards earning the money for the year's rent when it did fall due."

"Yes, you're right, of course." Jessica saw the bitter logic of that.

"In any case, my dear, with or without paying guests, you won't be in a condition to run this place for some while," Aunt Miriam pursued relentlessly.

"I thought perhaps you" — Jessica hesitated, knowing that she should not presume on past and present kindness — "I thought you might have grown to like it here and — and be willing to stay quite a long while."

"My dear Jessica, we can't possibly keep two homes running for an indefinite time!" her aunt pointed out, not unreasonably.

"No. I suppose not," Jessica agreed with a sigh, and then was silent.

There really didn't seem to be much else to say. She had made as good a struggle as she could to keep the home which she and the children loved, but luck had been against her.

Not, thought Jessica remorsefully, that they were not exceedingly lucky to have Uncle Hector and Aunt Miriam behind them. Their plight would have been serious indeed without their uncle and aunt. But — it had seemed at one time that hard work and determination and enthusiasm were going to be enough. And now, all because of an ill-timed expedition and a piece of bad judgment, her pleas to Uncle Hector and her appeal to Ford Onderley — not to mention her promising beginning with the Forrests — were all to go for nothing.

"It's not that I'm ungrateful for what Aunt Miriam offers," Jessica thought as she lay awake that night, going over and over the changed circumstances of her life. "It's just that I can't resign myself to leaving here. I *can't*. And I'm afraid the children will feel the same."

It would be her duty, of course, to point out the advantages of their new life and help to reconcile them to the change, but she was afraid it was a task for which she would have very little heart.

Indeed, when Judy paid her first visit to her home, Jessica found herself quite unable to tackle the subject, even though she had thought beforehand that it would be as well to make a few tentative hints.

But with Judy's arms clasped fervently round her neck, and Judy's voice saying over and over again how lovely it was to be home, how was it possible to start talking about leaving that home?

Instead, she hugged her little sister hard and said:

"It's very good to have you, my pet. And I'll soon be downstairs now, and then you shall come home for good."

"It's all right. I don't mind being at the hospital, really," Judy explained. "Not now that I can hop about and be allowed an occasional visit like this."

"How was this visit managed?" Jessica wanted to know.

"Oh, Mr. Onderley fetched me in the car, and he's undertaken to get me back there by six," Judy said. "It was his idea, ackcherly, and he talked Matron round."

"He's been most awfully kind over everything," Jessica said earnestly.

"Yes. I wish one could choose one's own uncles," Judy remarked. "I'd far rather have him for an uncle than Uncle Hector, wouldn't you?"

"Oh, hush! Uncle Hector's been very good, in his way, too," Jessica said hastily, not at all sure that she would like Ford Onderley for an uncle, and perfectly certain that he would hate having to regard her as a niece. Aloud she said, "He'd be much too young for my uncle, anyway."

"Yes, of course he would," Judy agreed. "How old do you think he is?" — because Judy was at the stage when the ages of grown-ups are a matter of passionate interest.

"I don't know," Jessica said truthfully.

"Well, I do."

"Judy! How do you know?"

"I asked him."

"How very rude and naughty of you," exclaimed Jessica. "Surely you know better than that, Judy."

"He didn't mind," Judy said, unabashed. "It was when I said it seemed funny that he was sort of looking after all of us and that he didn't seem old enough, somehow. And he said, 'Why, how old do you think I am then?' And I said, 'I don't know. How old *are* you?' and he said, 'Thirty, next birthday. Don't you think that's old enough for me to look after you all?' And I said, 'Yes.'"

"I see." Jessica bit her lip and smiled.

"He wants to come and see you, Jess."

"Why, so he shall, as soon as I'm downstairs," Jessica promised.

"But that's quite a long time yet, I expect," Judy objected. "Because you'd be surprised how funny your knees feel when you've been in bed a long time. Can't he come and see you here, now that you're up in a chair by the window? And you look very pretty in that chintz house coat, with your hair all brushed up like that."

"I suppose he could," Jessica agreed. "I don't know if Aunt Miriam has any ideas on the subject. She's a bit — funny about these things."

"What things?" Judy wanted to know.

But Jessica murmured, "Oh, never mind. I'll see what Aunt Miriam says."

"But he wants to know now," Judy objected.

"What do you mean — 'He wants to know now'?"

"Well, he told me to ask you when he could come," Judy explained. "And I'm to bring back your answer when he comes to take me away again."

"You'd better just tell him I'm not having visitors yet."

"But he knows that isn't true," Judy said firmly. "David Forrest goes to Oaklands to paint that stuck-up sister of Mr. Onderley, and he said something about coming with his mother to see you. And I don't think Mr. Onderley was very pleased."

"Nonsense. It's not his business to be pleased or otherwise," Jessica asserted briskly. "It's nothing to do with him."

"Well, when can he come?" asked Judy with praiseworthy persistence, for she was a child who was very difficult to sidetrack once she had her mind on a definite object.

Jessica laughed vexedly.

"Oh, all right. Let me see, what's to-day?"

"Wednesday. Visiting day," Judy said promptly. "Only I'm visiting instead of being visited."

"Well, he can come on Friday afternoon. And you'd better tell him I'll be very pleased to see him," Jessica said, finding that this was no less than the truth.

"Oh, yes, I'll tell him that. I'd have told him that anyway," Judy explained rather naïvely.

And then Tom and Mary arrived, and they all had a very gay and happy tea together.

"Oh dear, how quickly the time goes," sighed Judy when there was the sound of Ford Onderley's car coming to fetch her. "But I'll come and see you again soon, Jess." And she hugged her sister quite cheerfully as she said goodbye.

Then, with much laughter and trenchant advice from Tom, they negotiated the stairs together, though Jessica thought from the sudden cessation of the noise that someone came half-way up and carried Judy down in the end.

"I'm glad they find a broken leg and a crutch matters for laughter," she remarked dryly to Mary. "They really are the most extraordinary children in the things they find amusing. I must say the situation would strain my sense of humour a little."

Mary laughed.

"They're cheerful by nature, and I think Judy's finding it fun to feel well again. Anyway, the leg has mended excellently, you know, and the crutch is as much a joke as a support, I think."

"I dare say," Jessica smiled faintly, and wished

that her own recovery could have been as speedy.

When she announced Ford Onderley's projected visit to her aunt, that lady certainly put up her eyebrows and looked a little surprised. But she apparently thought the matter unworthy of an argument — or perhaps she considered that the desirability of an early discussion with him outweighed any other consideration.

She merely saw to it that Jessica was decorously buttoned into her tailored housecoat, and seated in a chair by the window, with a rug over her knees, in good time for the visit.

Jessica herself felt faintly nervous — though why, she hardly knew. Perhaps Ford Onderley always affected her a little that way, partly because she connected him with momentous decisions in her life and partly because she was never quite sure how he would react.

"He's a bit inclined to be a law unto himself," reflected Jessica. "I expect that's why he is rather unpredictable and alarming."

But there was nothing very alarming about Ford Onderley when, with a rather repressive expression, Aunt Miriam brought him upstairs that afternoon.

He looked cool and self-possessed, as usual, but his dark eyes rested rather kindly on Jessica as he took her hand, and he said to Aunt Miriam, almost accusingly:

"She doesn't look very strong yet."

"My niece has been very ill," Aunt Miriam pointed out austerely, "and I'm sure you will understand that we can't allow visitors to stay very long yet."

"That's all right, Aunt Miriam. I'll send Mr. Onderley away when I get tired," Jessica said, hoping her aunt would accept the implication that she intended to conduct the interview herself and did not require a third person there.

Evidently that was her visitor's idea too, because, as Aunt Miriam hovered, undecided, between her niece and the door, Ford Onderley showed polite but unmistakable signs of holding the door open for her.

Aunt Miriam, as she would have expressed it herself, knew when she was not wanted, and she retreated in good order, though with a somewhat dissatisfied expression.

Ford Onderley closed the door after her and then came back, to take a seat opposite Jessica and study her with the attentive concern of someone who had every right to do so.

Faintly embarrassed under this scrutiny, Jessica smiled and said:

"It's all right. I'm not fading away or anything. In fact, I'm improving daily. But first I must thank you for everything you've done, Mr. Onderley. You've been most terribly kind and —"

"Please don't." He smiled in his turn, and made a slight gesture of protest. "I haven't done a thing which hasn't been very easy to do. It doesn't amount to more than going to see your very good and entertaining little sister in hospital, and ensuring that you both have the small luxuries which everyone likes to give an invalid."

"No, no." Jessica shook her head. "I can't have it all dismissed like that. Even at the risk of embarrassing you — though I don't think you're very easy to embarrass," she added thoughtfully.

"Not very," he agreed.

"But, even at that risk, I must point out that you were first down the cliff to rescue Judy and me, that you took charge of everything for us from that moment, and that you've been more than kind and generous since. All that takes some thinking out, Mr. Onderley, as well as some time and effort in execution. So, in spite of your deprecating air, I insist on thanking you." And with a smile, she held out her hand to him.

He took it immediately, holding it warmly in his strong, firm clasp. But all he said was:

"Please don't accuse me of a deprecating air. I feel it would sit most unbecomingly upon any harsh landlord."

"Don't be absurd." She laughed. "I also insist on burying the harsh landlord myth, once and for all. And, anyway" — she bit her lip suddenly — "I'm afraid you won't be a landlord to us very much longer."

He glanced at her quickly.

"What makes you say that?"

"Why, Mr. Onderley, I'm afraid it must be obvious," she exclaimed with a little sigh. "You know that our — our arrangement depended on my being sufficiently well and strong to run this place and take paying guests. I don't want to exaggerate my illness, but I know it's left me horribly weak and — and, though no one admits it in so many words, I'm going to have a rather tiresome heart for a while at least. One of my visitors rather let that out. So it looks as though Uncle Hector's alternative scheme for our future will be the one to be tried." And she gave a rather sad little laugh.

Her visitor got up restlessly from his chair and, thrusting his hands into his pockets, walked slowly up the room and back.

"You know, don't you, that there won't be any question of rent until you get over this patch of ill-luck? So that if that's the only trouble —"

"Oh, Mr. Onderley, it isn't. But, in any case, you must see that I couldn't possibly accept such generosity."

"I don't see why not."

"Of course you do! You're a man of the world, and you once indicated very clearly that you had no sympathy with spongers — in which I agree with you."

"My dear child, the question of sponging simply doesn't enter into this," he exclaimed impatiently.

"Oh, but it would if we all elected to live on you rent-free. Quite apart from the comment which it would cause."

"I see no reason why there should be any comment on something which would be entirely between you and me, and not for public information at all."

She gave him a quizzically amused look.

"You haven't learned much yet about life round here, have you?" she said, almost indulgently. "If we continued to live on here without what I believe is called 'visible means of support,' I assure you there would be rich ground for speculation. But, in any case, I grant you that is of secondary importance. The real point is that we have not the slightest claim on you."

"Not that of friends?"

"My dear Mr. Onderley" — once more she put out her hand and took his, with a smiling air which suggested that she, rather than he, were in charge of the situation — "you have shown yourself much too good a friend for me to call you anything else. But, even with the best and oldest of friends, one only has a claim in a case of necessity. You know that as well as I do. Both I and the twins are being offered a perfectly kind and adequate solution of our problem by our only relations. The fact that we should much *prefer* to live here doesn't in the least entitle us to do so at your expense. You must see that."

He was silent for a moment, looking down at the hand which held his, and, glancing at him, she thought how mulishly obstinate his handsome mouth could look.

"You mean," he said slowly, "that I really have no right to offer a solution of your problem."

She flushed.

"Please don't think I resent your — your —"

"Interference." He supplied the word obligingly, with a rather grim little smile.

"I would rather call it interest," she replied firmly. "After all, it was I who first asked you to take a hand in our affairs. And, if I remember rightly," she added, with a demure smile, "I had considerable difficulty in persuading you to do so. I can hardly complain now if that — interest extends beyond the point I originally intended."

He acknowledged that with a short laugh and, moving away from her, stood leaning against the side of the window and looking down into the garden.

"So you propose to leave The Mead quite soon?"

She hated having it put into words, but there was no sense in being sentimental about the actual defining of the position.

"I think it is bound to be quite soon. Of course,

Uncle Hector will make the final decision now. There will be the question of finding boarding schools for the children — when Judy is well enough to go."

"Do they know yet?"

"No."

She could not manage more than the bald monosyllable, because the necessity of telling Tom and Judy about the changed future weighed heavily on her.

"They're going to hate it as much as you."

"At first, yes. But we shan't be the first people to have to adapt ourselves to circumstances we don't like."

She saw his mouth tighten obstinately again, and knew — if she had not known it before — that he was a man who reckoned to alter circumstances to suit his wishes.

There was an odd little silence. Then he straightened up suddenly and looked full at her.

"Have you realised that there is a way in which all these unpleasant changes could be avoided?" he said abruptly.

Jessica opened her eyes rather wide.

"No. I can't say that I have."

"You said just now that I had no right to offer a solution to your problem."

"Oh, I don't think I put it quite like that," murmured Jessica, but he brushed the interruption aside.

"Jessica, let me have the right to offer a solution. Marry me. And you shall stay on here — or, rather, at Oaklands — and neither you nor the children shall ever lack for anything."

CHAPTER SIX

JESSICA stared back at Ford Onderley in tense silence for a moment or two. Long enough for her to note, with exaggerated attention, the sound of a car approaching the house, passing and fading away into the distance again.

It was as though the sound intruded into a small, significant world which held only herself and Ford Onderley, and then retreated into that other, ordinary world from which, for a few minutes, she and the dark, purposeful man standing opposite her were completely isolated.

Then, as the last hum died away, Jessica found her voice and said, with a calmness which she herself found surprising:

"You didn't consider that last suggestion very carefully before you made it, did you?"

"Of course I did." For a man who was making a proposal, he sounded, she thought, incongruously impatient. "I never make suggestions without considering them. Why should you think I made this one without considering it?"

"I suppose — because one always thinks of quixotic suggestions being made on impulse," Jessica said with a faint smile. "And then as speedily regretted," she added as an after-thought.

"This isn't a quixotic suggestion, Jessica."

"No?" She opened her grey eyes wide.

"No. I should have asked you to marry me, even if all this trouble hadn't happened."

"Would you? But why?" asked Jessica with candour.

Something in that must have amused him, because he laughed — though a little vexedly, she thought.

He didn't reply directly, but with another question.

"Don't you know you're a very easy person to fall in love with?" he said, and again there was that touch of impatience, as though he resented having to explain something which surprised him at least as much as her.

"I hadn't thought of myself that way," Jessica told

him with truth. "And I — I'm not in love with you, you know."

She said that as gently as she could, not wishing to hurt someone who had been so good to her. But she thought, from the tightening of his mouth, that he was angered, rather than hurt, by the rare experience of having things not go his own way.

"I am willing to accept that," he said, "at present. I'm not so naïve as to suppose that all successful marriages start with romantic devotion on both sides. Perhaps mutual liking and respect count even more. I don't know. But, for my part, I can offer you most of the things that you and the twins think necessary to your happiness, and, in exchange —"

He paused for a moment, and she prompted him softly —

"Yes? In exchange —?"

"I shall have the woman I want for my wife."

At the way he said that Jessica experienced a curious little thrill, half alarm, half some emotion she could not define. And she thought: "What a curious word 'wife' is. It means nothing until it's applied to oneself. Then it means everything."

It was the first time, too, that anyone had called her a woman instead of a girl, and to Jessica that seemed of sudden and enormous significance.

"You don't — expect — a reply immediately, do you?" she said at last.

"No," he conceded. But she knew he was not pleased at the thought of delay, and she had a sudden, angry impulse to tell him that she would not be either bullied or bribed into marrying him.

Then she glanced up, and found his dark eyes fixed on her, with an expression of half-puzzled anxiety, and her heart softened unaccountably.

"It isn't that I want to keep you waiting, you know," she said quite gently. "But it *is* my whole life that I have to consider."

"I know." His expression changed, and he took her hand, touching her for the first time, she realised with surprise, since he had made his extraordinary proposal. "I'll be good to you, Jessica, within the limits of my disposition. And I promise you I will be good to the twins too."

Not every man, Jessica knew, would be willing to take on a couple of schoolchildren as well as herself. But Ford Onderley — shrewd assessor of a situation that he was — knew that through the twins lay his likeliest chance of getting what he wanted. A secure and luxurious life for herself might represent a minor temptation to Jessica, as to most girls. But the thought of providing for the happiness and security of the twins was something infinitely more valuable.

The eager impulse to thank him for his generosity was immediately checked by the cool reflection that, in this case at least, generosity and policy probably went hand in hand. So Jessica simply said, gravely and quite sincerely:

"I'm sure you would be very good to us all — Ford."

Perhaps he thought the use of his Christian name indicated a hopeful concession, because he flushed slightly — a rare thing with him — and said:

"How long will you want, to make up your mind?"

"You mustn't try to tie me down." Jessica spoke earnestly. "I promise not to take very long, but I refuse to be kept to a time limit."

"Very well."

She thought he was not at all used to having any-one say, "I refuse," to him, but, judging from his faint, grim smile, he found a certain astringent novelty about it.

Then Aunt Miriam came in, with tea and a general air of intending to speed up things a little. And, as she remained to see that the visitor did not outstay his permitted length of visit, there was no opportunity for further conversation of anything but a superficial character.

It was curious, and a little disconcerting, to have Aunt Miriam's remarks all tending to show that they would soon be gone from The Mead, and be making a fresh life for themselves elsewhere. No doubt she thought that by talking about the approaching change, she would reconcile Jessica to the idea more quickly.

But, with the incredible alternative now fixed in her consciousness, Jessica found it difficult to speak as though she too thought departure inevitable.

Consequently, conversation rather took the form of statements by Aunt Miriam, noncommittal murmurs from Jessica, and polite attention on Ford Onderley's part. But it was heavy going, and all three of them were glad when the party broke up.

After escorting their visitor downstairs, Aunt Miriam returned to collect the tea things and, glancing over her spectacles at her niece, she said severely:

"I hope you haven't been allowing that young man to put some other unsuitable suggestion before you, Jessica. You sounded to me as though you were still toying with some alternative to your uncle's very sensible plans for you."

"Ford Onderley didn't put any unsuitable suggestion before me," Jessica stated categorically. For surely even Aunt Miriam would regard marriage as a suitable suggestion.

"Well, I'm glad to hear it," her aunt said, though still a little sceptically. "I don't like him very much."

"Don't you, Aunt Miriam? Well, I do," Jessica replied dryly.

"Not such a good type as young David Forrest," Aunt Miriam asserted confidently. "Now, that's a *really* nice man, Jessica. The kind of man I should like to see you marry."

"Oh, Aunt Miriam!" Jessica laughed protestingly. But she felt unaccountably distressed as well. Perhaps because Aunt Miriam's remark, following so closely on Ford's proposal, threw into sharp relief the fact that David was indeed much more the stuff of which good husbands are made than Ford would ever be.

Not that she had ever entertained romantic hopes of David. At least, hardly any at all.

She had been too busy and too much occupied with immediate problems during the last few months to think along those lines. She had known that she liked having David in the house, that she was inordinately pleased about his wish to paint her, and that, in some indefinable way, she had regarded him as a friendly ally in any emergency.

But had she gone any further than that?

It was difficult to say now. And Aunt Miriam's inopportune comment only made her feel restless and troubled. For there was quite enough to make her decision difficult, as it was, without the introduction of the disturbing element of "It might have been."

"You've been up quite long enough," Aunt Miriam declared. "You're beginning to look tired and peaky, and the sooner you get back to bed, the better. I was afraid Mr. Onderley's visit might be too much for you."

"No, it wasn't too much for me," Jessica insisted. But she was glad to go back to bed, because, once she had installed her there (presumably, out of mischief), Aunt Miriam would be willing to go away and leave her to her own thoughts.

The moment the door closed behind Aunt Miriam's retreating figure, Jessica's thoughts — released from the necessity of dealing with Aunt Miriam's presence — fled back to the tremendous and significant fact of Ford Onderley's proposal.

Jessica knew that, until this moment, she had been deliberately putting off considering it. She had pretended to herself that the really important thing was to conclude his visit without her committing herself, to ensure that Aunt Miriam suspected nothing unusual, to secure for herself an opportunity for solitary thought.

Well, all those small, immediate necessities had been attended to. She now had her opportunity for solitary thought. And nothing stood between her and the momentous question: What was she to do about Ford Onderley's proposal?

The material advantages were, of course, so obvious that it was hardly necessary to go over them. He was rich, he was a man of known integrity, he was probably indulgent — in the way that dictators are sometimes indulgent, thought Jessica shrewdly — he was prepared to be a conscientious guardian to the twins, and, on his own admission, he loved her.

At least — Jessica paused and frowned as she tried to recall his exact words.

No, there had not been any exact declaration of love, now she came to think of it. He had merely said — almost reluctantly — that she was "a very easy person to fall in love with."

"It means the same thing," thought Jessica impatiently. But she was not absolutely certain that it did.

She lay watching the evening sunlight throw a slowly moving pattern across the bedroom carpet, and for a moment or two her thoughts wandered. Then the sound of Uncle Hector clearing his throat loudly in some other part of the house made her bite her lip with the easy irritation of the convalescent.

To have to live for months and months within sound of Uncle Hector clearing his throat! It was an unbearable thought.

Not, of course, that one decided life-and-death issues on trifles of that kind. But — how did one put up with the constant irritation of it?

"Don't be silly!" Jessica admonished herself quickly. "And, in any case, as soon as you get better, you'll start some training for earning your own living, and they'll be just as glad to see the back of you as you will be to escape."

Escape into what? she thought idly the next moment.

A girls' club? Lodgings? A bed-sitting-room of her own? Possibly a very tiny flat, if she were lucky. And that would be home.

Never again to know the exquisite relaxation of wandering through a rambling house. Never to have a garden of one's own. Never to know that, within call, were the two dearest people in the world — Judy and Tom.

"I suppose that escapade at the tarn will be the last expedition we shall have together," thought Jessica. "By the time I've made a success of things" — because her innate optimism allowed no real thought of failure — "and we can be together again, they won't be children any longer. They'll be just as dear, but they'll be different people and we'll have grown away from each other. Time doesn't stand still, and their years as children are so short."

With a pang, she remembered that, from their point of view too, the years as children were so short. They were not the kind to take kindly to boarding school, interspersed with holidays with Uncle Hector and Aunt Miriam. They would adapt themselves to that régime, of course, because they were good and cheerful children. But the lovely, carefree years they could have had would be gone and could never be called back.

But, if she married Ford Onderley . . .

Deliberately, Jessica tried to imagine herself running Oaklands for Ford — as his wife. And, as she did so, she recalled, for the first time, another significant figure in the picture: Angela.

Angela, she thought, would not be very pleased to welcome her as a sister-in-law. Nor, come to that, would Jessica have much pleasure in the relationship. But one had to bridge these differences in a marriage. And, presumably, however little she liked to abdicate, Angela would not expect to remain at Oaklands if her brother married.

But, absent or present, she would, Jessica guessed instinctively, be something of an enemy. That overheard conversation in the car had been a significant pointer to that. Angela would undoubtedly consider her an outsider who had had the effrontery to break into a tightly closed family circle.

"But I shouldn't be marrying Ford's relations. I should be marrying him — if I did take him on," thought Jessica. And then she wondered what other members of the family there might be, to approve or disapprove of her intrusion.

Since Angela had run Oaklands until now, she was presumably his nearest — or perhaps his only near — relation. That would simplify things.

But, in any case, all these considerations were merely minor ones. Jessica knew that she was weighing them carefully and with exaggerated attention because she was instinctively shirking the fundamental issue. Leaving the question of inlaws and an entirely new standard of life and even the twins out of account, what did she really feel about being the wife of Ford Onderley?

That was the real point. What would it be like to link her life and her personality to his in the strongest and most intimate bond that existed?

She moved restlessly against the pillows which Aunt Miriam had piled up so carefully, and thought, "How little I know about him, when it comes down to thinking of him as a life companion. And how little he knows of me, in spite of his air of certainty."

For a moment, panic overwhelmed her — as though the marriage were already an accomplished fact and there was no escape from sharing her life with a comparative stranger. Then she reminded herself firmly that nothing had yet been decided, and that the decision lay entirely with herself. No one was over-persuading her. No one would exercise undue pressure. It was for her to decide whether she were willing to take this incalculable risk for the sake of the twins and, to a lesser extent, her own material welfare.

"Many girls have married for less," she told herself, "and been very happy."

But what were "many girls" — or any other generalisation — when it came to considering one's own personal life?

No help at all. And advice would be of very little help, too. Whom could she ask for advice? Aunt Miriam? Unthinkable, quite apart from the fact that Aunt Miriam looked at life from an angle entirely different from one's own. Mary? No. Though Mary's advice would probably be well-balanced and affectionately sincere, it was impossible to put so much of Ford Onderley's private affairs before a near neighbour.

Whether she accepted his proposal or refused it, no one in the neighbourhood ought to be in full possession of the circumstances.

"She wasn't in love with Ford Onderley, you know, but she took him because he could do so much for her and the children."

Mary would never actually *tell* anyone that. But it would be disloyal to Ford if she gave anyone the power to think just that whenever meeting him.

No. It was something she would have to think out for herself, unassisted by any advice.

But, although she thought and thought until she fell asleep that night, Jessica arrived at no definite conclusion.

In the next few days, however, life was very much brightened for Jessica by one of those sudden accesses of health and strength which mark the real turning-point in any convalescence. Even the doctor — a cautious man — agreed that a trained nurse was no longer necessary. And, with the support — and under the elaborate direction — of Uncle Hector, Jessica was able to come downstairs and sit in the garden during the afternoons.

It was difficult not to feel that, with the return of strength, there might also come the return of old plans and hopes, now cast aside. But Jessica knew that, much better though she was, the point when she could support herself and the twins was still immeasurably far off.

Tom came every day to see her and, on the hospital's visiting day, Judy too put in an appearance. Somewhat to Jessica's relief, it was Mary, and not Ford, who brought her in the car.

"I can't stay, dear. I have to do a duty call for my papa," Mary explained. "But I'll call back later for the infant, and I dare say there will be time for a short chat then."

"Very well." Jessica smiled. And, as she watched Mary drive away, she thought: "I should lose Mary's companionship, too, if we went away from here."

"Do you think I ought to go into the house and say how d'you do to Aunt Miriam first?" enquired Judy, breaking in on these melancholy reflections.

"Yes. It would be best," Jessica agreed. While Tom said, without enthusiasm:

"I'll come and keep you company, if you like, though I've already seen her and Uncle Hector once to-day."

Judy, however, seemed to think she was quite capable of dealing with Aunt Miriam alone. So Tom withdrew temporarily to oil the garden roller with the aid of an oil can specially borrowed from Mary's sympathetic gardener. And Jessica was left alone to enjoy the sunshine and the mingled scent of the flowers and the hundred little sounds which go to make up a summer afternoon.

It was all very peaceful, and she felt faintly drowsy, as well as contented. Indeed, she had actually closed her eyes, when she suddenly became aware of an alien sound which had nothing to do with the peaceful pattern of the afternoon.

Hurrying, uneven steps announced the rapid and agitated return of Judy, while, mingled with them, were the unmistakable sounds of ill-suppressed sobs.

"Judy!"

Jessica opened her eyes as her little sister rushed up to her and almost literally flung herself upon her in a paroxysm of distress.

"It isn't *true* about our going away from here, is it, Jess?" Judy wailed. "It *can't* be true. Aunt Miriam says it is and that Tom and I have to go to boarding school. Oh, do say it isn't true!"

Inwardly cursing Aunt Miriam for having sprung this on her, Jessica hugged Judy tightly.

"Stop crying like that, darling. It — it isn't quite decided yet, and there's no need to get into this state."

"But there *is* need, if we're going away from here," cried the literal Judy. "What do you mean about its not being quite decided yet? Oh, Jess, I've been so looking forward to coming home. It's been nice at the hospital and they've been kind, but I wanted to come home all the time, only I wouldn't make any fuss, because you were ill. But it was so lovely now you were getting better. And then Aunt Miriam has to say this about our going away. And boarding school too! That means being separated from Tom, as well as you and home, because no one ever had the sense to have a boarding school for both boys and girls, did they?"

Jessica wilted a little under this spate of words —

every one of which seemed to throw into sharper relief the grey changes which were to come upon them all if Uncle Hector's proposals were to be followed out.

"Judy, we should have the holidays together," she began rather feebly.

"Where?" asked Judy quickly.

"Well — well, at Uncle Hector's home and —"

"Oh, Jess, how *awful!*"

"It's very kind of them to want us," Jessica pointed out, while she felt that "want" was being used in a comparative sense in this case.

Judy seemed to think so too, because she said candidly:

"They wouldn't want us at all. And why should they, anyway? People don't want each other just because they're relations. It's kind of them to have us because they *don't* want us. But being kind doesn't make things less awful."

The profound truth of this reduced Jessica to distressed silence for a moment, and at that point Tom came up to join them, wiping his hands on an oily rag, with every appearance of absorbed enjoyment as he did so.

But Judy swept him into the vortex of her own woe.

"Oh, Tom! There's Aunt Miriam saying we've got to go away from The Mead, and you and I are to go to boarding school, and Jess will live with them, and we'll only see each other in the holidays — at *their* horrid home, which is just a house in a street," finished Judy, arriving at the final detail of misery.

Tom, who took both his pleasures and his griefs more composedly than Judy, looked questioningly at Jessica.

"Oh, Jess! Is that true?" he said, and the one appalled question shook Jessica as much as Judy's flood of distracted eloquence.

"It — it isn't quite settled yet," she stammered, as she had to Judy. And Judy caught that up again.

"You said that before. What do you mean, Jess? What could prevent it? What *could* prevent it?"

Jessica looked from one painfully anxious little brown face to the other.

"Look here, children. It's perfectly true that we can't go on living at The Mead, but it's possible——" She drew a deep breath, found that she was trembling, and resolutely suppressed the fact. "How would you like to live at Oaklands?"

"Live—at Oaklands?" they gasped in chorus. And Judy added, "With Mr. Onderley, do you mean?"

Jessica meant so exactly that, that for a moment she could only nod. Then, realising that she had gone too far now to beat any sort of retreat, she said, as composedly as she could:

"Mr. Onderley wants me to marry him, and for us all to go and live there."

Again the twins registered acute astonishment, though Tom almost immediately recovered himself sufficiently to say with some complacence:

"What did I say? I *told* you I thought Mr. Onderley might ask you to marry him."

"Why, so you did!" cried Judy, genuinely impressed. And then, turning to her sister: "Oh, Jess, how simply splendid! Then we needn't any of us go away."

Tom, whose thought processes were a little more subtle, refrained from open jubilation until he had asked, somewhat anxiously:

"Do you *want* to marry him, Jess?"

Jessica quite distinctly recognised this as the moment when her real decision must be made, and, with hardly a trace of hesitation, she said:

"Why, of course, Tom. I wouldn't have told you about it, otherwise."

"Then what were you waiting for?" enquired Judy with joyous impatience, while her happy relief beamed from her. "Did you just want to make sure we liked the idea too?"

"Something like that," Jessica told her with a smile. And, throwing her arms round her sister in a passion of congratulation and relief, Judy cried:

"It's a *wonderful* idea, Jess! It couldn't be better."

"Do you like Mr. Onderley so much?" Jessica smiled at her curiously.

"Oh, yes." Judy dismissed that with cheerful positiveness. "Besides, it means keeping us all together and in the place we all like best. Oh dear, fancy my crying for nothing like that." And she scrubbed her tear-stained face with a grubby handkerchief.

"I think you'd better go and wash your face," Jessica said, surveying the rather disastrous results of Judy's activity. "But, Judy"—as Judy started off very willingly towards the house—"don't say anything just yet to Aunt Miriam or Uncle Hector. I mean—I'd better tell Ford first."

"Doesn't he know he's going to marry you?" enquired Judy, greatly intrigued.

"Yes, of course. At least—I haven't given him any final answer yet. But now I know you would both like it too, I'll tell him," Jessica explained. And, as she did so, she experienced that heady sensation which always goes with the burning of one's boats, however much one may doubt the wisdom of the action.

Fortunately, the twins were, like most children, quite prepared to take anything in their stride, once they had absorbed the salient facts. And they refrained from much comment on the new situation.

From time to time, Judy burst out with such vital questions as, "Do you think we'll be allowed to roll the lawn at Oaklands?" or "Will you be married in white? And will Mary be your chief bridesmaid?" But, on the whole, they were willing to wait upon events, once they had been assured that the peril of exile had been removed.

By the time Mary rejoined them, they were so used to the whole idea that Judy enquired quite naturally.

"Does Mary know?"

"Do I know what?" enquired the sharp-eared Mary. "I know most things that go on around here."

Jessica looked faintly put out, and Judy said jubilantly:

"Well, I don't believe you know *this*!"

"What's the mystery?" Mary looked amusedly from one to another.

"It—isn't a mystery, Mary. It's just that I'm—well, I'm going to marry Ford Onderley."

"*Just* that you're going to marry him!' cried Mary. "My dear girl, how sensational! I should call that front-page news, with no 'just' about it. When on earth was this decided on?"

"This afternoon," put in Judy quickly.

"Why, has Ford been here and proposed and gone away again all in the short space of time that I've been missing?" enquired Mary incredulously.

"No, no," Jessica laughed a little protestingly. "Judy means that she and Tom gave their consent this afternoon."

"And Jessica's still got to tell Mr. Onderley that it's all right," supplemented Judy obligingly, "so don't start congratulating him, if you see him."

"I won't," Mary promised, and gave a quick, curious glance at her friend.

Jessica flushed faintly under it, and hastened to explain further:

"I—wouldn't give a definite answer until—until I knew how the children felt about it, so——"

"Seriously, Jessica?" Mary interrupted with something like real protest. "Do you mean that your—decision about marrying depended on what the twins thought?"

"No, no. Of course not." Jessica saw that she was getting into deep waters, and knew that her shrewd friend was aware of the fact. "But, after all, it was a decision which would greatly affect the twins, too, wasn't it?"

"It was," Mary agreed, and her tone was very slightly grim. Then she added more briskly: "Come along, Judy. Hop into the car, there's a good child, or we shall be late. Go with her, Tom, and help her in."

Jessica recognised this perfectly well for a neat ruse to get rid of the children for a few minutes, and braced herself for the next question. As the children passed out of earshot, it came, with all Mary's uncompromising directness:

"Jess, you aren't just marrying him to provide a home for those children, are you?"

"No," Jessica said, with admirable composure. "I'm marrying him because I love him."

"Jess!" Mary looked, Jessica thought impatiently, quite ridiculously puzzled.

"Why not? He's terribly attractive, when you get to know him, you know. And he's been so wonderfully good to me."

"Yes. Yes—I know." Mary bit her lip doubtfully. "It's just—— Oh, you don't seem to have known him any time, and somehow I never imagined your falling for anyone like that. You have too much sense of humour and personality to be dazzled by the arrogant, good-looking sort. Don't think I'm speaking against him, Jess. I know he's been goodness itself to you and the kids. Only—oh, I suppose it's so obviously an advantageous match from every material point of view that a cynic like myself doubts the romance a bit," she finished with a laugh.

"You're not a cynic, Mary. You're incurably romantic, as a matter of fact," Jessica told her with a smile. "But it—it *is* a love match, and I wouldn't want you to think anything else."

"Well, darling, I only want to be assured that it's for your happiness, of course," Mary cried, and kissed her warmly. "A thousand, thousand congratulations, if this is really what you want. No one will be better pleased than I to see you happily married and settled here. I just—was afraid—for a moment——"

"Yes. I know. But there is nothing to be afraid about," Jessica assured her calmly. "And, Mary dear— do something for me, will you?"

"Anything," promised Mary in the emotional generosity of the moment.

"Ring up Ford for me, and ask him to come along and see me. I can't do it myself, because I still can't walk to the phone without Uncle Hector's arm and——"

"Yes, yes. I see Uncle Hector would be a disturbing element," Mary said understandingly. "Leave it to me, dear. I'll phone him the moment I've deposited Judy at the hospital. I must fly now, or she'll be driving the car off on her own and breaking the other leg."

And, with a wave of her hand, Mary ran off towards the car.

CHAPTER SEVEN

PRESENTLY Aunt Miriam came out and said—wasn't
Jessica cold and didn't she think it was time she came
in?

"No, thank you, Aunt Miriam. I'll stay just a little
longer."

Jessica sounded pleasant but determined, for she was
almost sure that Ford would come just as soon as he
received Mary's message, and she had no intention that
the situation should be complicated by his having to
pass Aunt Miriam's catechism before he reached her.

Her aunt looked a trifle dissatisfied, for she had come
to associate that particular tone of Jessica's with what
she called "obstinate and unpractical notions." But,
with a slight shake of her head, she went into the house
again. And a few minutes later Jessica heard the sound
of a car approaching.

She knew quite well it was not just a car. It was his
car. Not that she identified it by any special knowledge
of the sound—as Tom would undoubtedly have done.
She just *knew* that this was Ford Onderley coming to
hear her say that she would be his wife.

As he drew up at the gate, she sternly repressed a
shiver of nervous excitement, telling herself that Aunt
Miriam had been right, and that it was certainly grow-
ing too cold to stay out of doors.

And then he was coming across the smooth lawn
towards her, and she smiled. Because didn't every girl
have to smile when she was going to accept a proposal
of marriage?

"Mary Skelton rang up and said you wanted to see
me." He took her hand and stood looking down at her.
"Is anything wrong? Do you want something done?"

"Why, no, Ford." She actually laughed then and
slightly bit her lip. He was so very sure that if anything
went wrong, he was the man to put things right. If he
already thought he could manage all her affairs for her
when he had no special right to do so, what was he

going to be like when he considered her his complete concern?

But it was too late to think about that now. Her task at the moment—and suddenly she found it a difficult one—was to tell him of her decision.

She glanced down at the strong, rather fine hand which was still holding hers.

"I—I just thought it was time I gave you an answer to the question you asked me the other day." His grip tightened slightly and, she thought, involuntarily. "I spoke to the children about it this afternoon, because, of course, it does concern them too. And"—she picked her words carefully—"and that clarified my own ideas, and——"

"Do you mind skipping the details," he said with a certain impatient amusement, "and giving me the answer?"

"I'm sorry." She laughed again, a little nervously, and flushed. "The answer is 'Yes' of course. I thought you realised——"

"No. I never 'realise' anything about you," he told her a trifle grimly. "I find you quite unpredictable, and can make no clever guesses about you."

Even in that moment, she was surprised that anyone so simple and straightforward as herself should represent any sort of problem to Ford Onderley. But aloud she only said:

"Well, you don't need to guess any more about this. I—I will marry you, Ford. Thank you," she added, and then thought what an entirely ridiculous thing to say. Apart from the incongruity of it, she supposed it emphasised the fact that his proposal was the solution of a pressing problem, rather than any manifestation of romance.

Presumably he sensed that. Because he put his hand under her chin and tilted up her face—rather abruptly, Jessica could not help thinking, for a gratified lover.

"It's because of the twins, isn't it?" he said. Not accusingly, but as though they might as well have the position clear.

"No," Jessica said. "Not entirely." And somewhere,

at the back of her mind, a surprised flicker of consciousness registered this as true.

Then he bent down and kissed her, full on her mouth.

It was probably the first time in her life that Jessica had been kissed, in the full sense of the word. Her serious nature and her busy life had rather precluded fun and flirtations, and, except for her father's occasional and rather absent salutations, or Uncle Hector's decorous pecks, she could not remember having been kissed by a man before. And the touch of Ford's firm, rather possessive lips sent another slight shiver of excitement through her which, this time, she could not entirely repress.

"What is it? Are you cold?" he asked quickly.

And because that was the only possible reason to give, she said:

"Yes. I am a little. I've been out here too long, I think. But I—I wanted to have you to myself."

He gave her a quick smile at that, though she thought the faintly cynical comprehension in his eyes indicated that he knew it was a desire to dispense with Aunt Miriam's company, rather than any romantic urge, which had prompted her remark.

But he was still smiling as he bent down and picked her up out of the chair.

"Oh, Ford! That isn't necessary."

"No?" He looked down at her as he held her close against him. "It's what might be called a pleasing indulgence, then." And he carried her into the house.

Aunt Miriam was crossing the hall as they entered, and stopped short at the sight of what she evidently considered a slightly unseemly spectacle.

"What is it, Jessica? Are you feeling faint?" she enquired sharply, before even greeting Ford.

"No, Aunt Miriam." Jessica smiled with composure, though she felt a little foolish. "Ford was kind enough to want to save me the exertion of walking and——"

"My niece is quite able to walk now—with the assistance of her uncle," Aunt Miriam informed Ford austerely.

"No doubt. But I happen to like the idea of carrying

my fiancée into the house," he explained coolly. "And Jessica has just agreed to become my fiancée."

"Jessica!"

Aunt Miriam's exclamation was a peculiar mixture of dismay and congratulation—due, Jessica supposed, to the fact that, though she vaguely disapproved of Ford personally, she was quite unable to overlook the extraordinarily pleasant financial aspect of the match. After all, it was not every penniless niece who could be counted on to carry off the richest matrimonial prize in the district.

Again that slightly cynical gleam in Ford's eyes seemed to indicate a complete understanding of the situation, and Jessica reflected with amused apprehension that she was marrying a very perspicacious man.

Ford pushed open the sitting-room door with his shoulder and, carrying Jessica in, deposited her safely in an armchair opposite an astonished Uncle Hector. Like Aunt Miriam, he appeared to think it highly undesirable that Jessica had employed any means of returning to the house other than the support of his own arm, for his first remark, as he looked over his spectacles at them, was:

"If you had let me know you were ready to come in, Jessica, I would have fetched you."

"Yes, Uncle Hector. I know. But Ford was there, and it wasn't necessary to disturb you. You—you know Mr. Onderley, don't you?"

Uncle Hector said that he did. But his tone conveyed the fact that, up till now, he had derived little pleasure from the acquaintanceship. And Jessica gathered that he had by no means forgiven Ford for his dictatorial behaviour when she had first been taken ill.

Aunt Miriam by now had followed them into the room, and she said, "You had better tell your uncle, Jessica," in much the same tone she would have used for urging her niece to own up bravely to having broken her uncle's watch.

Jessica smiled irrepressibly, and then said gravely:

"Ford and I have just decided to get married, Uncle Hector. It—really isn't so—so surprising as Aunt

Miriam seems to think. Ford says I'm a very easy person to fall in love with and—and I think he is, too. So it really isn't so amazing that we want to marry, is it?"

Uncle Hector did not reply at once to this somewhat ingenuous statement. Employing his usual form of delaying tactics, he removed his spectacles, polished them at length, and then said:

"This is a very sudden decision, Jessica. And, while wishing you both extremely well, I feel bound to point out that marriage is not something to be embarked upon without forethought and consideration. I am afraid you are following your father's regrettable tendency to leap first and look aftewards."

"No, sir. You really do Jessica an injustice," Ford assured him dryly. "She has been thinking this over for several days—keeping me on tenterhooks meanwhile, I might say," he added with a smile.

Uncle Hector did not actually say, "And very proper too." But he glanced at his niece with something like approval.

"Well, if Jessica has given this matter serious thought, that does, of course, alter the case," he conceded. "What"—he cleared his throat tactfully—"what did you propose for the twins' future, Jessica?"

"Oh, they'll come with me, of course," she said quickly.

"I should like them to make their home at Oaklands," Ford stated unequivocally, and Jessica glanced up at him with a brilliant smile.

"Hm. I see," said Uncle Hector, and although both he and Aunt Miriam refrained from exchanging anything like a glance of profound relief, there was no doubt about it that a degree of geniality crept into their manner.

To do them justice, neither would have hesitated to put duty before personal convenience, but it *was* an enormous relief to see the future of their nieces and nephew being settled before their eyes, without the sacrifices which they had been gloomily, if conscientiously, contemplating.

"Well, of course," Uncle Hector said, "you and I

will have to have something of a talk, Mr. Onderley. I stand more or less *in loco parentis* to Jessica, though she is of age and entitled to make her own mista— that is, her own decisions."

"I hope she will never have cause to regard this as one of her mistakes, sir," observed Ford with a smile.

And Uncle Hector was gracious enough to say, "I think not. I think not."

He was not insensible to the subtle flattery of Ford Onderley's "sir." But that, in itself, would not have been sufficient to soften Uncle Hector. He thought his niece's choice of husband an odd one—the man was altogether too arrogant and apt to think he knew better than older and more experienced men—but Uncle Hector was no fool where essentials were concerned, and he recognised Ford Onderley for a decent, upright man. Beyond that, Jessica must judge for herself, and make—and pay for—her own mistakes.

Aunt Miriam's acceptance of him was a little slower —signalised by the fact that she did not ask the accepted fiancée to stay to dinner, but remarked firmly, on the other hand, that Jessica was obviously tired by all the excitement and had better return to her room.

Jessica raised no objection to this. Nor, except for a slight tightening of his mouth, did Ford.

He merely picked Jessica up again with that rather startling ease, and carried her upstairs to her bedroom. And this time she made no protest. It was nice, she thought, not to have to make any more effort. She seemed to have been making so many, ever since Judy had arrived that afternoon.

Only when he had set her down again did she realise that, as the happy fiancée, she ought to manage to say something about future plans. But all she could manage was—

"Are you—are you going to have a talk with Uncle Hector now?"

"About marriage settlements and future prospects, you mean? Yes, I expect so."

She had not meant anything of the sort, so she flushed deeply and said,

"No. I wasn't thinking of—of anything mercenary,

like that. I just meant—well, whatever Uncle Hector meant when he spoke of having a talk with you."

"That was what Uncle Hector did mean," Ford informed her amusedly. "And quite rightly, too. That and, I suppose, some sort of reassurance about my being a perfectly respectable person for his niece to accept as a husband. He's a shrewd old boy, your Uncle Hector. I find I rather like him, after all."

Jessica smiled faintly.

"Then you don't mind his heavy parental talk to you?"

"Good heavens, no!"

"And—after that?" She wondered if he would expect to see her again.

But apparently not, because he said:

"After that? Well, I expect I shall go home after that and break the news to Angela."

Another disquieting aspect of the situation presented itself then.

"Oh—she won't be very pleased, will she?" Jessica spoke with candour because she was too tired for polite pretence.

"At having to hand over the reins of government, you mean?"

"Partly that. And partly"—Jessica thought of the overheard conversation in the car—"partly that she just doesn't like me."

"She hardly knows you, Jessica. Or you, her."

"No. That's true. But what she knows of me she doesn't like."

He laughed—amused rather than put out.

"Angela would not have welcomed any wife of mine with open arms," he said, with a candour that matched Jessica's. "But she is quite intelligent enough to adapt herself gracefully to changed circumstances.

"Yes, of course. I—I don't want to make too much of the point. I don't even know why I raised it," Jessica said quickly. "I'll do my best, too, you know."

"Of course. Don't worry," he told her with that air of careless certainty which indicated so clearly that he was used to shaping things the way he liked them.

Then he kissed her and went away—leaving Jessica

Life was to revert, in some curious way, to the pleasant normality which had existed before her father died, and there was to be at least six months' engagement, during which she would live at The Mead with the twins, while she gradually got used to the idea that presently they would all transfer to Oaklands and—she could not escape the phrase—become the property of Ford Onderley.

"It'll be just like old times," declared Judy with a blissful lack of tact when the situation was explained to her. "I mean, it'll be awfully nice going to Oaklands later on, but I'm glad we're going to have the rest of the summer and autumn together at home first."

"I'm glad, too," Jessica said.

"And won't even Uncle Hector and Aunt Miriam be here?" enquired Judy hopefully.

"No. Now that I'm so much better, they feel they simply must go back to their own home and see to their own affairs," Jessica explained, keeping a restraining hand on Judy, who showed a tendency to leap with ungrateful joy.

"Linda and I will do *everything*, so that you needn't exert yourself a bit," Judy promised ecstatically.

"I'm sure you will." Jessica kissed her and laughed. "But I'm quite able to do some things now, and certainly able to attend to the general running of the place."

Even the cautious Aunt Miriam admitted this finally. And, with a mutual relief—which both sides strove manfully to conceal—she and Uncle Hector parted at last from their nieces and nephew, and took their way, with a considerable degree of staid joy, back to their own home.

"It's funny how lovely it is to see the last of nice people sometimes," remarked Judy with artless inoffensiveness when they had gone.

"Let's hope they're feeling the same way about us," Jessica said, with a smile.

And Judy said that, yes, of course there was their point of view too.

Then she and Tom went off to tea with a school crony, and Jessica was left to the luxury of having

The Mead on her own, except for the invaluable Linda.

She sat in the drawing-room, with its long windows framing a breath-taking view of the valley and the hills beyond, and mended the household linen, and thought how lovely it was to feel well again. Future problems and worries might exist. Indeed, did they not in the most fortunate and well-regulated of lives? But, for the moment, she was tranquil and she was happy.

Presently she heard the door-bell ring, and Linda's rather heavy footsteps cross the hall. And a few moments later, Angela—in an exquisite feather-weight green tweed suit and daringly absurd green hat which suited her to perfection—was ushered in by an obviously impressed Linda.

It was the first time she had come near Jessica since the engagement, and, though Jessica had tried hard not to see this as a deliberate affront, it was difficult not to remember it as she greeted Angela now.

However, Angela had her excuse ready—even if it was delivered in an extremely casual tone.

"You really must forgive my not coming to see you before," she told Jessica, more as an instruction than a request. "But just after Ford told me about the engagement, I went away on a visit, and I really haven't been back very long."

Jessica, saying nothing about the amenities provided by the Post Office and the telephone service, assured Angela that "it was all right."

"It's nice to see you now, though, and I'm so glad you came," she said, managing somehow to infuse cordiality into her tone. "You're the one person who can give me the best advice about how Ford likes things and——"

"He likes them managed with deadly efficiency and no fuss," cut in Angela in a tone calculated to make the most courageous quail before the task. "But Mrs. Curtis, the housekeeper, is very experienced and will keep you right. And, as for managing Ford himself, you seem to have done that very well already."

It took Jessica a moment to control her anger sufficiently to ignore the obvious implication. But she was determined that Angela should not provoke her into a display of nervous temper.

"I know it sounds trite to say it, but I can't help hoping, Angela, that you and I will be good friends when we get to know each other better," she said quietly.

"It's not very likely." Angela ran a cool, speculative glance over her. "We are not at all the same type. But, of course, we shall contrive to be reasonably agreeable to each other. And, anyway, I shan't be very much at Oaklands."

"Won't you?" Jessica said, and controlled her relief and pleasure with difficulty.

"No. I never intended to make my home there, once Ford married."

"I see."

Jessica hesitated, then, deciding that plain speaking might suit this cool, unfriendly girl best, she said:

"You're not very pleased about Ford's marriage, are you, Angela?"

Angela shrugged.

"In Ford's place, I should have chosen differently," she said. "But that's his business, not mine. And I suppose, in many ways, it suits you both very well. It certainly provides a comfortable and luxurious home for you and those two children. And, on his side—I suppose you know Ford was desperately in love with someone else who turned him down?"

"No," Jessica said coldly. "I didn't. And I don't think you had any right to tell me anything so intimate about your brother, since he had not chosen to tell me himself."

"But men are so odd in their confidences and their reticences. After all, you had a right to know. It puts you in a false position if you suppose yourself to be the object of some wild devotion which doesn't exist," Angela pointed out a little maliciously. "It's just as well for you to know that Ford expended all that on some-one else and so, I suppose, felt free to indulge in some quixotic gesture over a make-do marriage."

"You certainly have a talent for puttings things as unpleasantly as possible, Angela." Jessica spoke with a

117

coolness which matched her visitor's, though she was pale and her eyes looked dark because the pupils had grown so large.

Angela laughed slightly.

"Oh, no. I believe in looking facts in the face myself. If not, they are inclined to look *you* in the face, which is much more unpleasant. I imagine you are enough of a realist to know that for yourself."

"I hope so," Jessica said curtly.

"And, anyway, what is there so unpleasant about what I have said? The basis for this marriage is not such a bad one, if you're both truthful with each other, and accept the fact that there's not much romance on either side. You're marrying, quite frankly, for money, and he is marrying because—well, because most men want to marry, and he knows he can't have the woman he does want, so——"

"What makes you so confident of the fact that I'm marrying for money?" inquired Jessica icily, while she gripped her cold hands together.

"Oh, my dear"—Angela laughed, as she stood up and drew on her gloves, presumably to indicate that the call was at an end—"if not, why didn't you marry that nice artist, David Forrest? He was mad about you, and could have made you reasonably comfortable, I suppose. Only, of course, he's only about a quarter as rich as my brother. No doubt you chose very well, all things considered."

CHAPTER EIGHT

JESSICA remained quite still, watching Angela deliberately smooth each finger of her gloves as she put them on, taking as much time as possible over the task.

She knew quite well that the last disclosure had been made with the intention of provoking her to exclamations and questions, and, for a moment, she was so furiously determined not to play Angela's game that she actually managed to ignore what had been said.

But, as her unwelcome visitor turned to go, she knew she could not leave things there, and she spoke, quickly and coldly.

"What did you mean when you said that about David being—being mad about me?"

Angela glanced back over her shoulder with slightly raised eyebrows and a mocking smile.

"Didn't he tell you?" she enquired incredulously. "He told me."

"What do you *mean*—he told you?" Jessica was startled into immediate retort that time.

"Why, you know"—Angela turned to face her once more—"when someone is painting your portrait, as David was painting mine, and there's nothing much to do for quite long periods except talk, you become surprisingly confidential. Maybe he said rather more than he meant to, but—it seems you were quite the only girl, so far as he was concerned. You're not going to tell me this is news, are you?" she added scornfully.

Jessica did not answer, for surprise and dismay and some other quite unidentifiable emotion were struggling in her heart. And after a moment Angela said softly:

"Didn't you know?"

"He—never said anything about it," murmured Jessica.

"I told you—men are the most extraordinary creatures," Angela declared with a light laugh. "But you were a bit dumb too, if I may say so, not to guess for yourself."

"How could I guess?" Jessica still spoke more to

119

herself than to Angela. But, as her visitor shrugged, as though to say that anyone but a fool would have guessed, she shook off her momentary bewilderment and added sharply: "After all, it may be your guesses that went a little wild. You simply say 'it seemed' that —that David was fond of me. Perhaps you jumped to too hasty conclusions."

"No," Angela said. "David was quite categorical. But I shouldn't really be saying all this to you, should I?" Her greenish eyes gleamed with faint malice. "Ford would hardly thank me for putting such ideas into your head. You'd better just remember that my brother is much the bigger catch of the two, and certainly much better qualified to take on a couple of schoolchildren along with his wife. Now I simply must fly. I'm having tea with the Cavendishes and I'm late already."

Jessica made no effort to detain her and, on a delicate wave of expensive perfume, Angela departed, leaving her future sister-in-law as agitated and perplexed as she had meant her to be.

When she had gone, Jessica sat absently pleating the tablecloth she had been mending, and tried to put into perspective what Angela had just said.

It made no difference, of course. She was engaged to Ford, who had undertaken to provide a home for her and the children, and any other man's feelings for her were of purely academic interest.

At least—no, one could not use the phrase "academic interest" where someone as warm and vital as David was concerned. If he had spoken before Ford . . .

But he had not spoken. Not to her. She had nothing to go upon but a reported conversation with Angela.

It was understandable, of course. Her relationship with David, before that unlucky accident upset everything, had been one of delightful and developing friendship, when anything—or nothing—can happen. There had been no apparent need to hurry things. How could David, or anyone else, have guessed that Ford would make his astounding proposal?

Why *had* he made it, come to that? thought Jessica.

Probably Angela, with her disagreeably cynical explanation, had been very near the truth. He could not have the woman he wanted, and so the girl who intrigued and amused and commanded a certain amount of respect from him would do instead.

It was time he married, anyway, and to combine a quixotic gesture with a piece of cool-headed expediency would undoubtedly appeal to his sense of paradox.

Yet if David had spoken first . . .

"I mustn't start thinking along those lines," Jessica told herself a little wildly. "He didn't speak, and he's gone way, and by the time I see him again it will be almost time for my wedding. Anyway, Angela may have made half of this up. She's a born mischief-maker"—for Jessica had no illusion now about her future sister-in-law—"and obviously meant to make me miserable and worried about this."

And then it came to her, with something of a shock, that, only if her own feelings were involved, could there be any question of her "making herself miserable." Why, then, was she so deeply moved?

Of course no decent girl wanted a good friend to make himself unhappy over a hopeless passion for herself. But need it go deeper than that?

Jessica had not found any satisfactory answer to these questions by the time the twins returned, with their affectionate but insistent demands on her attention.

"We met Ford on the way home," Judy explained. "We've finally decided that we'll call him Ford, too, by the way. He doesn't like being Uncle anything, and we don't like it either. After all, he's a brother-in-law really, isn't he?"

"Going to be," amended Jessica a trifle curtly.

"Well, going to be. It's the same thing," Judy replied, with a pleasant disregard for the tricks that Time and Fate can play. "He says we can call him Ford, so that's all right. And he also says we're all to come over to Oaklands as soon as possible, because we haven't even been over the place yet."

"Is that an order?" asked Jessica with a most uncharacteristic flash of irritation.

Both the children gaped slightly.

"It was an invitation, not an order," said Tom, recovering himself first, while Judy added frankly:

"Aren't you feeling very well, Jess?"

"I'm quite all right, thank you." Jessica felt and sounded contrite. "I—I just thought you put the invitation in a funny way."

"Did I?" said Judy, and began to re-examine her own wording with such laborious attention that Jessica said hastily:

"It doesn't matter, dear. I've got it straight now. When are we to go to Oaklands?"

"Ford said you were to decide that," Tom explained in a tone which added quite clearly: "See how little of an order it was!"

Jessica smiled involuntarily.

"Almost any day next week will do for me," she remarked pacifically. And then added: "I expect Angela had better decide what will suit her."

"Oh, Angela!" exclaimed Judy, and made a face. Which so exactly expressed all that Jessica herself had been thinking of that lady that she could not find it in her heart to reprove Judy. She merely said conscientiously:

"Well, Angela will be our hostess at Oaklands, after all."

"Only for the time being," Judy stated with naïve satisfaction. "*You'll* be the hostess there soon, won't you, Jess?"

"I don't think I'd emphasise that fact for the moment," her sister said dryly.

"No. But it's nice to think about it," Judy said, and obviously meant it.

The next day Ford came himself, to repeat the invitation in a more exact form, adding—entirely on his own initiative, Jessica could not help thinking—that Angela would be very glad to see them all at Oaklands.

So it was arranged that, after church on the following Sunday, they should all three go to Oaklands for lunch and stay for the rest of the day. Put in that way, the invitation assumed a slightly formal character—which was perhaps what Angela had intended—but the twins accepted, for their part, with unconventional whoops of satisfaction which rather destroyed any suggestion of formality.

"Are you *so* pleased to be seeing Oaklands at close quarters?" Ford looked amused.

"Oh, yes. It's much the biggest and most interesting place in the district," Judy explained. "Besides, it's going to be home," she added with a touch of artless pleasure.

"Yes. It's going to be home," Ford agreed, and, putting a hand on Judy's head, he ruffled up her brown hair, teasingly but not without affection.

Watching them together, Jessica thought: "The children have a surer touch with Ford than I have myself. I wish I felt as much at home with him as they do."

Ford, however, seemed to consider himself quite at home with Jessica, for, when the children had gone off on their own affairs, he said with extreme frankness:

"Angela came to see you yesterday, didn't she? Is that why you're grave and thoughtful to-day?"

"Ford—*no*!" exclaimed Jessica. But she blushed, partly because of the unexpectedness of the question and partly because she was aware that she was not being entirely truthful. And, to cover her confusion, she countered with: "Why do you ask? Did you expect her to say something to upset me?"

"Expect? No, that would be too strong a word," he conceded. "But being related to Angela doesn't blind me to the fact that she can be something of a trouble-maker when she likes. I just wondered——"

"Ford, what an odd way to regard your own sister," said Jessica who, coming from a devoted family herself, was inclined to suppose that all brothers and sisters regarded each other with a partial eye.

"But why be unrealistic about one's relations, simply because they are relations?" asked Ford amusedly. "Angela and I get on quite amicably, and I wish her very well. But I am not unaware of her faults, and I'm certain she is very well informed on mine," he added with a laugh.

Jessica found herself wishing that such frankness from him might be answered with equal frankness from her. At that moment, she would have given much to be able to tell him of the two disclosures which Angela had made yesterday. But he was, of course, the last person to whom she could mention these, and, with a slight sigh, she turned away and looked out of the window, as though absorbed in watching the twins who were out on the lawn as usual.

"What is it, Jess?"

She was aware suddenly that he was standing close behind her. And then he lightly put his arms round her. So lightly that, although in the first reaction she stiffened slightly, oppressed by all the untold things which stood between them, after a moment she relaxed against him, from the sheer relief of having someone on whom she could almost literally lean.

"There's nothing the matter," she said slowly and without much conviction. At which he laughed softly and kissed the top of her bright head, rather as he might have kissed Judy.

"Darling," he said, "there's quite a lot the matter. This is rather an odd marriage which we propose to make, and there are several features about it which worry you profoundly. But you can't talk about them to anyone, because you have no one to consult. Isn't that it?"

Jessica turned her head and looked up at him, half fearful and half relieved at his penetration. His face was quite close to hers but, for once, it was not his handsome, cynical mouth which she noticed most. It was the strangely kindly look in his dark, penetrating eyes.

"Well, it—it is a bit that," she found herself admitting.

He sat down on the wide window-seat and drew her down beside him, but so that she could still lean against him and did not need to look into his face unless she wanted to.

"Listen to me, Jess. I'm perfectly well aware that the most important thing in the world to you just now is to provide a happy home and background for the twins," he said calmly. "There's no need to reproach yourself about that. It's natural and it's right. I don't imagine there's anything of the grand sacrifice or any other melodramatic feature about your marriage to me. But the plain fact is that if you had not the responsibility of the twins, you probably would not have chosen to marry me. Isn't that right?"

"Ford!" She moved disturbedly against him. "Do you really think it helps either of us to have things quite so much in black and white?"

"Yes," he said, with a touch of his old cynicism. "I think it helps you, although it shocks you slightly, too." But he softened what he was saying by touching the curve of her cheek with his lips. "I'm willing to accept the position exactly as it stands—as I told you when you first agreed to marry me. What I did not add then, but which I will add now," he said slowly, "is that you may take your own time over everything. Do you understand? I shall not force the—the pace of this marriage beyond anything which you yourself want. Until you wish otherwise, you can regard me, if you like, as simply the man who provides you and the twins with a home."

"But, Ford, that—that's unfair!"

"It's the way I want it," he retorted coolly. And then added dryly: "No one but a fool tries to regulate his married life by what is fair or unfair."

Jessica turned suddenly and put her arms round him.

"Oh, I wish——" Then she stopped and put her head down against him, without saying what it was that she wished.

"What do you wish, Jess?" He was rather unnaturally still as he looked down at her.

"I wish I knew whether it's kindness or cleverness that makes you say the generous things you do."

He laughed at that with real amusement, and kissed her.

"Allow for a little kindness in my composition," he told her teasingly, "and I dare say you can put down the rest to the fact that I'm a wily fellow."

"I don't think that's the right proportion at all," she retorted with energy. "I think you're really generous and rather a darling. Only, of course, you're clever too and—and——"

"Time my generous impulses well?" he suggested.

Which was so exactly what Jessica meant that she laughed and kissed him, without actually replying.

"Well, my dear, look at it whichever way you like," he said. "Only try not to feel scared and trapped." A slight movement from her showed how surely he had guessed her feelings up to now. "We may not be starting with a wonderfully romantic basis for our marriage, but it's not an insecure one, you know. We ought to be able to build something successful and happy on it."

"I hope so," she murmured. And then added earnestly: "I'll try very hard, you know."

"Yes. I know you will." He smiled. "Don't try too hard, or you may wreck it that way."

"Oh, Ford!"

"All right. I'm only teasing you." He touched her cheek amusedly, and she instinctively drew rather close against him again. "As a matter of fact, there is only one thing which could wreck it absolutely."

"What's that?" She didn't move from her comfortable position against him, because she thought he was still teasing her.

"If you were very much in love with another man."

She was terribly glad, in that moment, that she had not been looking up at him, and he could not see her face very clearly. Not that she was "very much in love with another man." Only—there was David, and that revelation of Angela's yesterday, and all the disturbing conjectures and reflections which inevitably followed on it.

Yes. She was glad Ford was not actually looking at her as she said quite steadily.

"I'm not very much in love with anyone else."

"If you like, you can leave it at 'not very much in love with anyone,' " he told her with a laugh, seeming rather to enjoy the fact that his frank acceptance of the situation shocked her.

But, surprisingly, she made no answer in words. Only put her arms round him again and hugged him rather convulsively. And he refrained from asking her why—possibly, of course, because this was one of his "clever" moments.

Church on the following Sunday morning was, Jessica was very much afraid, regarded by the twins merely as a "curtain-raiser" before the visit to Oaklands. Certainly they were ready in good time, looking rather unnaturally clean and tidy, and their behaviour on the whole was decorous. But obviously their thoughts were elsewhere, judging from the glances which they sent towards the Oaklands pew where Ford and his sister attracted a good deal of surreptitious attention.

Judy, who had a taste for what she called "the jollier hymns," joined very heartily in most of the singing, but during the sermon she sat and regarded Angela with such speculative interest that Jessica wondered very much what was going on under her brown thatch. As for Tom, he was actually guilty of exchanging incomprehensible signs with Bob Parry, who occupied a respected position in the Choir, owing to his sweet soprano voice rather than to any standard of Christian behaviour.

Jessica frowned and shook her head at Tom, who promptly brought the sign conversation to a close with a particularly hideous grimace, and after that looked moderately attentive. But she was aware that there was an indefinable current of excitement in their pew that morning, and that she herself was by no means immune.

After all, she doubted if her attention were any more on the sermon than Judy's. For one thing, she was conscious that she herself was attracting some of that surreptitious local attention which concentrated mainly on the Onderleys.

Everyone knew about her engagement to Ford by now, and she was regarded with the mingled respect, envy and surprise due to one who had carried off the best matrimonial prize in the district. It was inevitable that people should glance from him to her with various expressions indicative of wondering how she had "done it."

Ford Onderley was not a frequent attender, and everyone was glad of this nice, cosy opportunity of examining him at leisure. As, in addition, his fiancée was also present, they provided between them a most

127

interesting morning, and food for plenty of future speculation.

If Ford found all this something of an ordeal, he certainly showed no signs of doing so, and Jessica could only hope that her air of calm detachment equalled his.

Afterwards, when they met outside the church, in the slowly moving stream of the departing congregation, he kissed Jessica and drew her arm through his as though they had been engaged at least a year. And his matter-of-fact acceptance of the situation steadied her and made her feel less self-conscious.

Several people came up to tell her (with genuine feeling) how glad they were to see her recovered, and they added their good wishes on her marriage, and achieved an introduction to the interesting fiancé.

Ford put himself out to be charming to everyone. Which was just as well, because Angela's aloof air did little to create any feeling of friendliness. On the other hand, of course, it provided ample opportunity for extending the discussions which later took place over half a dozen lunch tables, because it was obvious to all that "the sister isn't any too pleased, my dear," which added piquancy to the situation.

On the way to Oaklands, Angela and Jessica both sat in the back of the big car while the twins, after a lively discussion on the question of who should go in front, both managed to cram in beside Ford.

This left Jessica feeling rather unpleasantly isolated, but she managed to make polite conversation during the short ride. Or, at least, enough of it to prevent Ford from feeling there was a significant silence behind him.

When they arrived at the house, both the children hopped eagerly out of the car and stood regarding Oaklands with satisfaction.

"It's even bigger and nicer than I thought," Judy declared. And it was with difficulty that she was persuaded to come indoors before exploring the full delights of the grounds.

As they entered the wide, impressive hall, Jessica very clearly recalled coming there that first evening to interview her unknown landlord and, glancing at

Ford, she thought that he too was remembering the same occasion, because he smiled at her as though they shared some amusing and rather pleasant recollection. And, curiously, that made her feel very much at home.

The children, though impressed with the grandeur of a house quite outside their previous experience, were not slow to voice their interest and approval. To most people their naïve expressions of pleasure and pride would have been quite inoffensive. But Jessica saw that they profoundly irritated Angela, and she was glad to leave the twins downstairs with Ford when her hostess took her upstairs.

Angela led the way to her own suite of rooms, with the remark:

"This is really my part of the house. I have my own sitting-room, as well as my bedroom and dressing-room. I like it that way, because Ford quite often has people who don't specially interest me."

As Jessica glanced round the beautifully furnished and decorated rooms, she could not help feeling that Angela might well hate parting with them. And, if her sister-in-law had been almost any other type, she would most eagerly have urged her to continue to regard this suite as hers.

But her common sense—as well as what Ford had said—told her that it would be asking for trouble to allow Angela to have a permanent footing in the household. So, feeling rather mean, she contented herself with remarking on the beauty of the rooms, and then turned to the mirror to comb her hair.

"You have very pretty hair," remarked Angela, watching her. And Jessica reacted immediately to what she thought was the first sign of friendliness.

"Yes, it's quite a decorative shade, if you're careful what colours you wear," she agreed. "I think your hair's lovely, and you can wear nearly anything with that very dark shade."

Angela accepted this without comment, and merely said:

"Is your hair really that colour?"

Jessica laughed.

"You don't think I'd bother to dye it at my age, do you?"

"You might. Or, at least, have it touched up. I thought you might have heard that Ford has a predilection for red-heads," she added, so casually that it was a moment before Jessica took in the full implication of that.

"Angela, what an awful way of putting it!"

Jessica still managed to keep her voice on a note of amused protest.

"Oh, I didn't mean that he runs after any girl who has that shade of hair," Angela conceded. "I just meant that when he does admire one, it seems he chooses someone with your coppery red colour."

"I see."

Jessica refused to turn round from the mirror, but she could see Angela reflected in it, and, at that moment, she pointed carelessly to a photograph on a side table and said:

"She had just the same shade of hair."

It was impossible not to turn round then and regard the photograph, though at least one could achieve an expression of polite interest instead of distasteful apprehension.

"She's very beautiful," Jessica observed courteously, looking at the lovely, clear-cut profile of a girl who obviously belonged to Angela's world rather than her own. "Who is she?"

"Your predecessor," Angela said with an expression which would have been teasing on anyone else, but which on her was extraordinarily malicious.

"Do you mean Ford was engaged to her?" enquired Jessica coldly.

"Oh, no. She took someone else," Angela explained. "She's the girl I was telling you about."

"I see," Jessica said again, and managed not to show that she thought Angela quite hateful. But she could not help adding dryly: "Is that why you keep her photograph here?"

Angela laughed—perhaps because she was pleased to know she had got under Jessica's skin.

"Oh, no. She's a friend of mine. Paula Dryden and

130

I were at the same finishing school together. She's often been to our London house in my parents' lifetime. She was very much one of our 'set,' and used to be staying with us sometimes when Ford came down from college for the vacation."

Jessica was very nearly trapped into saying "I see" again. But she remembered, just in time, that it was the standard reply when one was completely non-plussed, and managed to change it into,

"Well, she's certainly lovely enough to attract anyone."

She knew perfectly well that Angela was deliberately creating an impression of a closed social ring, where impecunious girls who got rheumatic fever and couldn't pay their rent had no right to intrude.

Angela probably guessed, with uncanny penetration, that Jessica felt anything but confidence in her role of Ford's fiancée, and if she *could* be persuaded that she would always feel an outsider. . . .

"Are you ready?" Angela's voice sounded cool and polite, and Jessica knew that the gloves were on once more.

"Yes. I'm ready," she said. And they went downstairs together.

Over lunch, Jessica was glad of the chatter of the twins, even if it did irritate Angela, for at least it gave her an opportunity of remaining silent sometimes and relapsing into her own thoughts.

One knew, of course, that Angela was trying to make everything as difficult and alarming as possible. But, even allowing for that, the situation was full of unpleasant possibilities. If Ford really *had* been very much in love with one of his own set, it was not specially surprising that he chose to go outside that set for a "second-best"—to link his life with someone who knew nothing about the previous affair.

But, though she might answer very well, as a temporary novelty, how was the "outsider" going to measure up to Ford's usual associates later on?

In a panic-stricken wave of revolt, Jessica thought, "Oh, I wish I needn't marry *anyone*!" and she felt childishly like crying. Only, of course, one had to go on being pleasant and social, and, above all, to conceal from Angela the depths of one's frightened misery.

Presently she recovered sufficiently to glance in Ford's direction. He was answering some eager question of the twins, and his smile was rather indulgent, so that Jessica caught her breath in a little gasp of something like relief.

How was it, she wondered, that anyone so positive and dictatorial as Ford could also be so strangely reassuring at times?

And at that moment he turned his head and smiled at her, and she thought, "If Ford loved one very much, one would feel perfectly safe about nearly everything."

Perhaps Angela intercepted the glance and thought it was time a new turn was given to the conversation, because she said abruptly,

"If you've all finished, would you like to come and see David Forrest's portrait of me?"

"Oh, yes!" they all three exclaimed with some eagerness, because David had been a great favourite with the twins as well as with Jessica, though Judy privately thought he had shown lack of judgment in choosing to paint Angela.

Angela led the way into a light, rather austerley furnished room, where the portrait of her stood on an easel near the window, and they stood and regarded it with varying degrees of judicial attention.

It was Tom who finally said, "I say! I'd no idea David was so clever!" Which exactly expressed what Jessica had been thinking.

It was not only that the painting was technically very beautiful, nor even that David had caught Angela's exact expression of aloofness and pride. It was as though he had very slightly lifted the veil from the inner Angela and, without in the least detracting from her beauty, had shown that inimical streak in her which made her wish her fellow creatures ill rather than well.

"It's a wonderfully clever study," Jessica said tentatively at last. And, to her astonishment, Angela replied:

"Yes. I'm delighted with it."

It was, Jessica thought, the final tribute to David's art that he had shown so much to the intelligent observer without disturbing the complacency of his model. To Angela there was nothing repellent about the portrait, any more than there was about herself.

"I've only one or two minor criticisms to make," she was saying now. "I want that background lightened a little, and a shade more brilliance in the dress."

"I suppose he will do that when he comes back in the autumn?" Jessica said.

"No." Angela smiled slightly, as she regarded the portrait. "I've suggested that he comes and stays at Oaklands for a short visit and makes the alterations. I think there will be plenty of opportunity while that tiresome mother of his is doing what she calls 'settling up.'"

"Do you mean David's coming up here again to stay quite soon?" It was Judy who eagerly asked the question which Jessica wanted to put.

"Yes. I think so." Angela glanced at her brother. "If we could persuade him to stay long enough, he might do that portrait of Jessica that he talked about."

"What a wonderful idea!" Judy was hopping up and down on what she called her best leg.

Jessica wanted to say that it was not a wonderful idea at all—that it was a horribly clever and trouble-making idea, thought up by Angela with a very special purpose in view. But she knew she was already paler than she should be, and that any protest from her would draw surprised attention to her.

And Ford—for once not so clever as usual about reading his sister's thoughts—said:

"Yes, it is a good idea. I'll see what can be done about it."

CHAPTER NINE

DURING the rest of the visit Angela made no further reference to David or his portrait. Indeed, she was rather surprisingly sociable and pleasant, and went up a good way in the innocent estimation of the twins.

To Jessica there was something faintly menacing about this change of front, however. There was a subtle suggestion that the victor could afford to be gracious, and she could not help wondering just what unscrupulous victory Angela believed herself to have achieved.

But it was useless to worry unduly about impressions or conjectures. And, in any case, there were other things to think about during this first real visit to Oaklands.

Ford, having sent the children off to explore the grounds on their own, took her over much of the house, consulting her wishes about various alterations to be made, and generally making her feel very much the future mistress of the place. He introduced her to Mrs. Curtis, the housekeeper—a rather severe, but obviously efficient woman—who, whatever she might have thought privately, accorded Jessica every courtesy due to an employer.

On the whole, Jessica gathered that she was approved—possibly because she showed some real knowledge about household management, and yet was willing to defer to Mrs. Curtis's evident experience in the running of this particular house.

"Besides," thought Jessica, with a secret flash of amusement, "in her place, I'd rather work for me than for Angela!"

Not until they returned home that night—after a visit which had, on the whole, been less of an ordeal than Jessica had expected—did the subject of David come up again. And then Judy said innocently:

"It'll be nice having David back here again, won't it?"

"Very nice," Jessica agreed.

"I wish he could come and stay here, instead of at

Oaklands. I'm sure he'd like it better," Judy declared.

"But Angela has already invited him to Oaklands," Jessica pointed out, thinking it unnecessary to go any further into the impossibility of David staying at The Mead now.

"Still, he'll be coming over here a good deal, if he's doing your portrait." Judy consoled herself with this reflection. "I bet he'll come as often as he can."

"He may not stay long enough to do my portrait this time," Jessica said. "If he only has time for a short visit, he—he'd much better leave it over until he comes again."

"But you'll be getting married almost at once and there'll be lots of fuss and things to do," Judy objected. "Though, of course," she added, as an entirely new and brilliant thought struck her, "he could paint you in your wedding dress then. That'd be *marvellous!*"

Jessica felt she could think of few things less agreeable than the idea of David painting her in her wedding dress—in the circumstances. But, with admirable self-control, she merely said David might consider that altogether too formal, and wasn't it time Judy went to bed?

It was. And even Judy had to admit the fact.

So the twins kissed her good night and went away, and Jessica was left to reflect at leisure on the events of the day.

She thought a great deal about the difficulties that would arise if David came back, feeling as he did, and saw her daily. And she thought as little as possible about Paula Dryden, with whom Ford had been so much in love.

Not, of course, that she was jealous of Paula. Why should she be? Not even that she felt possessive about Ford. It was just that she didn't want to think of him very much in love with someone else. Her mind instinctively turned away from the idea that, in mind and spirit, he had belonged much more to a girl from Angela's world than he would ever belong to her. It was quite understandable, and there was no need to explain it further to herself.

During the following week Ford had to go way on

business. And, in the sense that life immediately reverted to the blessed normality of the days before she had known either Ford or David, Jessica had to admit that there was an element of relief in having him absent.

Sometimes, if she took care not to glance at the ring on her left hand or to go near her father's study, she could have imagined she was back in the old days when, as it seemed to her now, she was both heart-free and carefree, and had no greater worry in the world than the ordinary domestic worries attendant on keeping house for a couple of unexacting children and an absent-minded parent.

"It's pure escapism to go on pretending about the past being present," Jessica told herself. But occasionally, when the children were at school and she could sit in the sunny garden sewing, while Linda hummed tunelessly over her work in the kitchen, she allowed herself to dream lazily of the blessedly uneventful past, and pretend that some unspecified miracle might bring those days back again.

It was after one of these pleasant reveries that she awoke one afternoon from a half-doze, to see David coming across the lawn towards her. And—more because he recalled her so sharply to present problems than because she had not heard any sound of a car— she exclaimed with quite disproportionate surprise,

"Why, David! How on earth did you get here?"

"Didn't you know I was coming?" He was amused and, she thought, quite aware that she had been half asleep. "Angela kindly invited me to stay at Oaklands, and I arrived last night. The rest of the journey I accomplished on my own two feet. How are you, my dear?"

"Oh, I'm fine now, thank you." Jessica had recovered herself. "Sit down and I'll get Linda to bring tea out here."

But Linda—who had always approved of "that nice young Mr. Forrest"—was already signalling in a somewhat unorthodox way to indicate that she would bring tea out on to the lawn.

"She has already risen to the occasion," said David, who had stayed quite long enough at The Mead to learn

Linda's simple sign language. "Stay where you are, Jess. You still look as though you could do with all the rest and leisure you can manage."

Jessica smiled. David always made one feel so well looked after. That was partly Mrs. Forrest's training, she knew. But it was also due to David's endearing thoughtfulness.

"Tell me all the news," she begged. "How is your mother, to begin with?"

(What she really wanted to know, of course, was how far Angela was concerning herself in their affairs. But this could only be discovered indirectly.)

David thrust his hands into his pockets, stretched out his long legs and grinned.

"Mother's having a wonderful time," he asserted. "She says she simply doesn't know which way to turn, which is her idea of heaven. And, to my certain belief, she has already reduced one strong, manly house agent to tears."

Jessica laughed.

"Dear David, how absurd you are! But I wonder your mother was able to spare you if there is so much to do."

"You don't understand my mamma at all, if you can say that," David assured her gravely. "She positively likes struggling with difficulties single-handed. You see, she is what is known as a wonderful woman, and it pleases her no end to have opportunities of proving to herself and others that she still remains a wonderful woman. When anyone says, 'Dear Mrs. Forrest, I don't know *how* you do all you do,' that person is Mother's friend for life."

"So she didn't mind your coming up here again without her?"

"No more than she always minds my slipping her apron-strings for a little while," David said with smiling frankness.

"Oh, David——"

"Yes?"

"Nothing. Except that you're very nice about the situation. Most only sons with—well, with slightly possessive mothers either resent the fact and cut loose

137

entirely, or else they succumb absolutely and become ciphers. You steer such a nice middle course with seeming ease."

"It's not quite as easy as it looks." He still spoke with the same good-humoured candour. "But it's well worth the effort. On the one hand, Mother remains very happy and satisfied most of the time, and, on the other, I usually have my own way over anything that matters very vitally to me. Like coming here again, for instance."

"Had you a—a special reason for wanting to come back here?"

"Yes, I had."

"I meant—apart from finishing Angela's portrait."

"Yes. I meant apart from that too."

"I did a certain amount of guessing," Jessica admitted, and found that her heart was beating uncomfortably fast. Not, to her surprise, with happiness but with a sort of uncomfortable agitation.

"That was clever of you, Jess," he said. "I thought I'd managed to keep my feelings pretty well to myself."

She was silent again, remembering that she had really done no guessing at all of her own. She had merely been told by an over-informative Angela. But one could not explain that.

And then he said quietly:

"What chance have I?"

Jessica felt her mounting dismay overwhelm her. If she had expected him to broach the subject at all, it had not been in this abrupt, over-simplified way. He was speaking as though Ford simply didn't exist—as though the question of the twins' future did not exist—as though she were perfectly free and might consider an offer from him, quite unaffected by the fact that she was wearing Ford's ring on her finger. And, in that moment, Jessica thought less of David than she had ever thought before.

He had no right to say, "What chance have I?" as though that were the only issue. And, since he had insisted on saying it, there was only one—equally over-simplified—reply to make, and she made it:

"I'm sorry, David. Not much chance, I'm afraid."

He took it quite well, she thought, considering that he had come all the way from London to ask that question and receive her answer. She saw his mouth tighten in an unfamiliar way. But he made no protests or pleas. He simply said, almost lightly:

"Well, I thought I'd try my luck, anyway."

"Yes. Of course."

More than anything else, she felt profoundly uncomfortable, and it was with extreme relief that she saw Linda coming across the lawn with the tea-tray.

It was amazing how useful trivialities could be in a moment of crisis. Virtually, David had proposed to her, implying that she might turn down Ford, and all his generous offers for the future, and she had refused him—all in the space of a few minutes. And now, here they were passing cups of tea, sending Linda back for a missing jam-spoon, chaffing her (or, at least, David was) about the amount she seemed to think they were able to eat, and generally behaving as though no vital matter had been put to the test and rejected.

Even so, Jessica could hardly hope that he would let the question go at that. When Linda finally returned to the house, they would surely revert to the subject—and even now she was turning her broad and uncompromising back on them.

Jessica braced herself for the coming discussion. And, as she did so, she heard the latch of the gate click and, glancing across the garden, she saw to her unspeakable relief that Mary was coming towards them.

"Oh, Mary dear! You're just in the nick of time," she cried with almost unnatural joy. "I mean—Linda's just this minute brought out tea," she added a trifle lamely.

"I pride myself on good timing," Mary said. "David! How lovely to see you. When did you get here?"

And in all the questions and explanations necessary to bring Mary up to date in the history of the Forrest family, Jessica felt that the earlier topic of conversation had been safely shelved, at any rate for the time.

That was one of the nicest things about Mary. She could be relied on to carry the burden of any conversation, and to be the amusing centre of it. And Jessica noticed that David, too, seemed delighted with her presence, and to direct most of his remarks to her. Perhaps he was as relieved as she herself that the tension could be relaxed and an unconscious third person be used, in order to bring back a safe degree of impersonality to their relationship.

Presently the twins returned from school, hungry and full of local news. And, after that, there was certainly no opportunity for intimate discussion.

"Ford's back," Judy announced. "We saw him driving up from the station."

"Did he stop?" With a perfectly steady hand, Jessica retied the hair-band which was slipping from Judy's tousled head.

"Oh, yes. And he said to tell you he'd either be up or ring up this evening. It depended on how much work he found waiting for him when he got back to Oaklands."

"Very well."

Jessica thought suddenly that she didn't want him just to ring up. She wanted to see him. Not because she had anything special to say. But—it was more than a week since she had seen him.

She could, of course, stroll over to Oaklands herself, once tea was over and the twins more or less settled down to their homework. But Angela would be there—and David. It might be difficult, and she certainly did not want to wound David's feelings further by thrusting the spectacle of herself and Ford as an engaged couple before him.

However, she realised at that moment that Mary was, quite unconsciously, solving half the problem for her:

"Why don't you come back and have dinner with us?" she was saying to David. "Daddy will be delighted. He approves of you. Or, rather, I should say he has a sort of wondering respect for you."

"Has he?" David seemed both gratified and amused by this. "How's that?"

"Well, you see, he belongs to the school of hard-headed business men who think that art is something in inverted commas, quite divorced from ordinary life. He simply can't get over the fact that you actually make a lot of money out of it and talk common sense about business. It's rather like finding that a performing seal has a taste for mathematics."

"Thanks a lot for the comparison," David said. "I ought to be wounded to the depths of my sensitive soul. But as I'm not, I will accept your invitation with pleasure."

"I wish you *were* a performing seal with a taste for mathematics," Judy remarked. "Then you might help me with my geometry homework."

"On the contrary, I should probably just clap my flippers in a superior way and balance an isosceles triangle on the tip of my nose," retorted David promptly. At which Judy laughed so immoderately that she was able to take a more cheerful view of her evening's tasks.

"I do like David," she said when he and Mary had said goodbye and gone off to engender wondering respect in the bosom of Mr. Skelton. "Sometimes I like him so much that I almost wish you could marry him instead of Ford."

"Well, I can't," Jessica stated with what Judy thought unnecessary snappiness.

"No, I know. If he'd just wait a few years until I grow up, I might marry him myself," was Judy's further suggestion.

"He won't be able to wait," observed Tom soberly. "Someone else'll snap him up long before then."

"Yes. I suppose so," Judy agreed, and reluctantly and very slowly she began to take her homework books from her satchel.

Jessica got up.

"I think I'll walk over to Oaklands and see Ford," she said. "You'll be all right, won't you? I'll be back in time for your supper."

"Yes, we'll be all right," Tom assured her. But Judy took it upon herself to add:

"But Ford said *he* was either going to come over or ring up."

"Yes, I know. But I think I'll go over to see him, anyway."

"Very well," said the twins, in what Jessica suddenly identified as tactful unison. And, to her amusement and slight irritation, she saw them exchange a significant glance as she left them.

"Little idiots!" she thought affectionately, as she ran upstairs to change her frock. "They think I'm so much in love with Ford that I can't keep away once he's returned home. I didn't know they had so much romantic imagination."

And she laughed a good deal as she changed into the grey-and-green patterned frock which had just come home from the dressmaker. Then she stood in front of her mirror and examined her reflection with critical attention. Not only to see whether the dress suited her personally—of that she felt reasonably confident already —but to see whether it conferred on her that indescribable quality of chic which was, no doubt, the natural attribute of Angela's friends. Of Paula Dryden, for instance.

Wide, rather anxious grey eyes stared back at her at first. But the reflection was, on the whole, a reassuring one. The beautiful wide sleeves, caught into tight wristbands, the cleverly cut skirt, which fitted so slenderly over her hips, but swirled into satisfying fullness at the hem—these gave what could only be described as an "air" to the dress. And, with a little toss of her head, with its red-gold crown of hair, Jessica decided that she was not such an insignificant successor to the glamorous Paula Dryden.

It was a warm evening, and she wore neither hat nor coat as she set out from the house, followed, as she was well aware, by the speculative gaze of her young brother and sister, who were only too glad to allow their attention to wander from their lesson books to the window.

She chose the longer, but pleasanter way, through a small wood, but most of the way she could keep the road in sight, because it was on a lower level, so that she would be able to see if Ford came along it by car from Oaklands.

No sound of a car broke the evening stillness, however, and as Jessica strolled along, she was free to follow her own train of thought.

Inevitably, this turned on her conversation with David that afternoon, and the feeling of which she was chiefly conscious was surprise at her own reactions.

Ever since Angela had first put it into her mind that David was in love with her and that she might have had him instead of Ford, Jessica had been wondering uneasily whether it were he that she really loved. Or, rather, whether she had been in the process of falling in love with him when everything had been so cruelly destroyed by her illness and Ford's precipitate proposal.

Because she had seemed cut off from David's love, and forced to take instead whatever Ford had left over from his infatuation for Paula Dryden, the unattainable had appeared sweeter than anything which she already had. And, though she had been anxious to do only what was right to the man who had been so generous to her, she had supposed it would have to be at the expense of much suppressed heartache.

And yet, when David had put things to the test—though certainly not in any way she had anticipated—her reply had been unhesitating. And it had not been accompanied by heartbreak and resignation. Only by distress and embarrassment on behalf of a very dear friend.

"Of course, I'll always feel affectionate and a bit sentimental towards David," Jessica thought, with self-frankness. "It's impossible not to, because he's so attractive and so dear. But if Ford is not *the* man in my life, nor is David." And then—"But I hope he won't be here very much. If things don't go well with me and Ford—and how can they always?—I don't want to have the tempting presence of 'the other man' who loves and understands. Even David's tact and diplomacy wouldn't be equal to carrying that situation off without danger. Oh, why can't I have a straightforward engagement and marriage, like other girls, instead of involving myself in a sort of ready-made triangle?" thought Jessica with a sigh.

Then she remembered the earlier references to triangles that evening and giggled a little and decided there was no need to take too tragic a view of the future. Ford had told her not to worry. Ford had told her that she might take her time over everything to do with this marriage And Ford—was coming towards her through the trees at this moment, and she forgot her other reflections.

"Hallo!" She waved to him, and he quickened his pace.

"Hallo. Didn't the twins tell you I'd come over to see you this evening?" He took both her hands and kissed her.

"Yes. But they also said you might only phone, and I thought I'd like to see you, anyway."

"Did you?" He was smiling down at her. "What did you want to see me about?"

"Nothing—special. I just thought it was a long time since I'd seen you."

"Oh, Jess, did you?" He laughed and put his arm round her. "Isn't this a new dress?"

"Um-hm. Like it?"

"Very much. It suits you."

"Ford, is it—is it smart?"

"Of course," he said carelessly. "Everything you wear is always smart "

"Oh, it isn't!" cried Jessica, gratified beyond expression. "Do you really think so?"

"Of course," he said again. "It's the way you wear your things. You have the smartest, trimmest figure I've ever seen, and you hold your head in the way only tall, queenly women usually hold themselves. It's enchanting on a smallish girl. When you walk down the village street, you look like a pocket empress."

"Oh, Ford, how sweet of you!" Jessica exclaimed and flung her arms round him.

At that, he laughed more than she had ever seen him laugh before, but he held her tightly against him.

"Is that the sort of sugar you like?" he said teasingly. "Just plain, unadulterated statement of flattering fact."

"No, darling, really——"

"What did you call me?" he said, smiling down at her.

"It—it just slipped out. I do call people 'darling' sometimes," Jessica explained, flushing slightly.

"Well, don't you go calling anyone else 'darling'

in future," he told her, and gave her a quick, hard kiss. "You keep it for me "

"All right," Jessica was surprised to hear herself say: "But, Ford, it wasn't just gratified vanity that—that made me so pleased, you know."

"Wasn't it? Nevertheless, I like to think I detect a little healthy, human vanity in you," he told her amusedly.

"Well, there is that too, of course," she admitted. "But when you said *such* nice things, it made me feel that I should be able to hold my own as your wife, and —and I want to do that."

"Against me, you mean?" He looked puzzled.

"Oh, *no,* I can do that all right," Jessica asserted, at which he looked greatly amused again and not displeased. "No, against all your own set who—who are probably very different from me."

"They aren't so real, and, on the whole, are not so intelligent, if that's what you mean," Ford said judicially.

"But they probably have a—a worldly finish that would make me rather country-cousinish by comparison," Jessica suggested anxiously.

He laughed.

"Don't attach too much importance to that, Jess. Manner is of rather little importance, provided there is something worthwhile behind it. It's only when there is nothing much to support the surface manner that the possessor has to pretend it has an exaggerated importance."

"Yes. I know that's true, really," Jessica agreed. And she secretly wondered how anyone so clear-sighted could have found all that he wanted in a woman in Paula Dryden. Unless, of course, Paula was quite unlike her friend, Angela, and much more human than her photograph had suggested.

"Come back to Oaklands with me now," Ford said. "I have something I want to show you. Something I got for you while I was in Town."

"For me? Do you mean a present?"

"Yes. A present."

"Oh, Ford, how sweet of you. What is it?"

"You wait and see," he told her. And, at his amused and indulgent tone, she suddenly recalled wishing that she could be as much at ease with him as the children— and it came over her that, this evening at least, she seemed to have achieved that happy state.

They took their time strolling back to Oaklands, and he kept his arm round her. He told her something of his business trip, and seemed amused and pleased that she was interested.

"Do you have to travel a good deal, Ford?"

"Oh, yes. Sometimes further afield than this country. Why? Do you want to come too?"

"I'd *love* it!" cried Jessica. "Do you—do you mean that I may?"

"Why, certainly, if you want to. Once the twins have got used to regarding Oaklands as their home, there's no reason why we shouldn't leave them in charge of some competent person like Mrs. Curtis."

He seemed, Jessica thought, to have looked ahead a good deal, and to have visualised a fairly detailed picture of their life together.

"It would be wonderful," she said slowly, and she meant it. For to travel with Ford would be to travel without anxieties or worries. He was the sort of man who ruthlessly smoothed out difficulties in any country and any language, thought Jessica amusedly.

When they reached the house, instead of going in by the front door, he took her round to the back and pushed open the big sliding door of the garage.

"Come and see for yourself," he said with a smile. And Jessica, who had stood back a few paces, came forward then and looked in interestedly.

The big saloon car was standing there—which probably meant that Angela was at home, thought Jessica passingly—and beside it was Ford's own racing car. But, in the very ample space remaining, there also stood another car which Jessica had not seen before. An elegant little wine-coloured coupé with shining metal-work, which seemed to beam with the pleased consciousness of being the very latest thing in small luxury cars.

"Ford, how lovely! It's new, isn't it?"

"Quite new."

"Is it yours?"

"No. Yours."

"Ford! *Mine?* But I couldn't—I mean—is *this* the present?"

"Um-hm. This is the present." He seemed both amused and pleased at her joy and astonishment. "I'll teach you to drive."

"You needn't. I can drive already. But I never, never hoped to have a car of my own." She was flushing and paling. "I can't imagine—— Oh, Ford! you shouldn't spoil me so terribly. I—I haven't really done anything to deserve it." And she turned and hid her face against his arm.

"Why, darling"—his voice was unexpectedly gentle —"why should you do anything to deserve it? We're not going to reckon things on that basis, you know." And he dropped a kiss on the top of her head. "I think you need a car, to save you as much exertion as possible. And, in any case, I like to give you a car," he finished, as though that in itself were really quite sufficient reason.

She laughed a little unsteadily and hugged him.

"It's the most wonderful present, Ford. I hadn't imagined anything remotely like that. I thought perhaps a handbag or—or a clip-on or something. But a *car!* Oh, it's lovely." And she affectionately stroked the shining bonnet.

"I'll bring her over to-morrow, and we'll get your licence and you can try her out," he promised.

"Yes. But I want just to sit in her for a moment now," Jessica insisted.

So she got into the driving seat, and he sat beside her and explained the mechanism, and also the beautiful shining gadgets which marked it so indisputably as a luxury car.

They were still sitting there, laughing and talking, when a shadow fell across the entrance to the garage, and Angela came in.

"Oh, I thought I might find you here," she said, addressing her brother first. And then—"Hallo, Jessica."

"Hallo, Angela." Jessica opened the door of the

car and leant out. "Have you seen my car? Isn't she heavenly?"

"Yes, it's a beautiful car," Angela agreed quite politely, but without enthusiasm, and Jessica thought she probably considered that her brother had been wasting his money.

"Well, what is it?"

Ford had got out of the car now, and stood looking down at his sister, like a man who had been interrupted in some very pleasant task but was in too good a humour to resent even that.

Angela held out an open letter which she had in her hand.

"I've just had this letter from Paula. She's very upset because her engagement's been broken off. I'm not really surprised. I always knew Edward wouldn't suit her."

Jessica was aware that there was a moment's complete silence before Ford replied, and when he did speak, his voice was very cold.

"I'm sorry," he said formally, "but I don't know that it's really very much our concern.'

"Of course it is, Ford! Paula is one of our oldest friends," Angela retorted. "Besides, I've made it my concern. I've wired to say she must come here for a while. A complete change is the best thing when you've had an emotional upset."

"I don't think you should have done that without asking me," her brother said extremely curtly. "I would rather not have Paula here."

"But, Ford, how unreasonable of you! She will be here as my guest, not yours, and I've always been free to invite my own guests to Oaklands." Angela, for once, sounded almost plaintive. "I can't put her off now, you know."

"No. I realise that," Ford said grimly. And, as he turned to hand Jessica out of the car, she saw that he looked pale, and as near angry as she had ever seen him.

CHAPTER TEN

HAVING once made her sensational announcement, Angela took pains to be extremely affable—not only to her brother, but to Jessica as well. She admired the car, said she thought it was a good idea that Jessica should have one of her own, and finally pressed her to stay to dinner.

Jessica was glad to be able to refuse—on the perfectly legitimate plea that the twins were expecting her home.

"You do indulge those children, don't you?" remarked Angela in the tone of one commending Jessica's sentimental feelings while deploring her lack of judgment.

"No," Jessica said, a good deal nettled. "I don't think I do. They're very good children, and stand on their own feet well for their age. But, if I've told them I'll be home, I don't like to disappoint them without a very good reason."

"Of course not," Angela agreed with deceptive softness. "But I think you'd go a *little* far in sacrificing yourself for them," she added reflectively. "Don't you, Ford?"

"I don't know what you're talking about," retorted her brother impatiently. "Come along, Jessica. I'll run you home."

There was no suggestion of their using Jessica's own lovely little car, and somehow the bloom had gone from the pleasure of that gift. Not that Jessica regarded her car with any less breathless admiration, nor that she felt any less grateful to Ford for his generous impulse. But the intrusion of Angela and, by implication, of Paula too, had sounded a jarring note against the very perfect harmony which had existed for a few happy minutes between her and Ford.

She hardly knew whether she was relieved or disappointed when he said he would not come in. Immediately her nervous fears told her that he was more agitated than she had thought about Paula's coming, while she welcomed the chance of being left alone to consider the new and disagreeable situation which Angela had created. And though she thanked him again very eagerly for the car, she thought he looked a little sombre as he kissed her—as though to him too the car had become of secondary importance.

The twins greeted her cheerfully, and Judy thrust her books into her satchel with a thankful *"That's done!"*

"Did you get your geometry right in the end?" asked Jessica sympathetically.

"Well, I finished it," said Judy with a nice distinction of meaning. "In a way," she added.

"What do you mean—'in a way'?" Jessica felt bound to enquire.

"Well, I got an answer," Judy explained. "Only it seems very improbable."

"Maths answers are more often improbable than not," her brother assured her consolingly, and Judy seemed content to leave the matter there.

"Anyway, I shall get a few marks for trying," she remarked cheerfully.

Jessica felt that she ought to point out that this was a rather poor standard of performance at which to aim. But, just as she was about to say so, Judy diverted her attention by asking, "Any news from Oaklands?"

"No. What news should there be?" Jessica spoke quickly and a trifle defensively because she was very conscious of the news there had been about Paula. Then she recalled Ford's gift to her, and added hastily, "At least—yes, there is some news. Ford has given me a wonderful present. What do you think it is?"

Judy made various wild guesses, ranging from a puppy to a diamond tiara. But Tom just thought deeply for a few moments and then said solemnly:

"Is it a car?"

"Yes," Jessica said, a good deal surprised. "How did you know?"

"A car!" screamed Judy delightedly. "What sort of a car? Do you mean a car for your very own?"

Jessica smiled and nodded, while Tom forged on with his own deductions.

"I bet it was that ripping red coupé he was driving up from the station. When I saw it, I knew it was new, and I didn't see what Ford needed with a new car himself, and he wouldn't give one to anyone but you, so I wondered even then."

Jessica looked at her brother with something like respect, while Judy cried:

"Oh, I *wish* I'd noticed it more!"

"Well, you'll have plenty of time to notice it now," Jessica pointed out soothingly. "Now eat up your supper."

Judy proceeded to do so, though with many pauses to ask searching questions about the car, while Tom interjected highly technical enquiries from time to time —none of which Jessica was able to satisfy.

"I say, you don't know much about your own car, do you?" Judy said rather reproachfully at last.

"Well, I didn't have very long to examine it," Jessica objected.

"Didn't you? Why not?"

"Well——" Jessica hesitated, and thought of Angela coming in and spoiling the pleasure which she and Ford had been finding in each other and the car. "Oh, Angela came in, and we were talking about other things, you know."

"More interesting things than the car?" enquired Judy sceptically.

"She wanted to speak to Ford about a friend of hers who is coming to stay."

"Oh," said Judy, and was so obviously going to ask further interested questions that Jessica was extremely relieved to see her gaze shift suddenly to the gate and that part of the path which could be seen from the window. "Here are Mary and David back again," she exclaimed in a tone of pleased speculation.

Jessica followed her glance with some surprise, and saw that this was indeed the case. David, she thought, might quite well have found his way back, with the idea of further discussion, or Mary might have come over, as she so often did, for a casual chat. But that they should have come back together, like this, seemed to call for some specific reason.

The front door always stood open at this time of year, and Mary was sufficiently at home at The Mead to wander in and out as she pleased. After a moment, her voice called from the hall:

"Hello! Anyone at home?"

"Yes. We're all here," cried Judy. And, jumping up, she ran to meet Mary in the doorway. "Hello, Mary. I'm glad you looked in again. What *do* you think? Ford has bought Jessica a car. Isn't that a marvellous present?"

"Marvellous," agreed Mary, standing in the doorway and smiling round gaily on everyone. "But Jess isn't the only one to have a present to-day, Judy. David has brought *me* a present—and what do you think that is?"

"Goodness, I can't imagine!" declared Judy, finding it too much to be asked to guess twice in one day.

So Mary just laughed and held out her left hand, and they all saw that a very lovely sapphire ring glittered on her "engagement" finger.

"Mary, how lovely!" shrieked Judy, while Tom said, rather aggravatingly, "I'm not a bit surprised."

"You horrid child! Of course you are," declared Mary cheerfully, while Jessica could only say, "Darling, how—how amazing!" and then look past Mary to where David was standing, smiling, with the satisfied air of a man who knows he has done a very good day's work.

She got up then, and came to Mary, to throw her arms round her and kiss her, and exclaim with the utmost sincerity, "I'm so glad, dear! I'm so terribly glad!"

And this was nothing less than the truth. For, however puzzled she might be by the situation—in view of what she had thought until this moment—she knew, in that moment when she saw Mary and David standing there together smiling, that her two dearest friends belonged inevitably to each other, and that they were going to be doubly dear because they were together.

"Well, Jess"—David smiled and held out his hand to her—"you didn't give very much for my chances, did you? But it seems I was luckier than either of us guessed."

"Oh, David!" With a little gasp, Jessica seized the

hand he held out to her. "What an *idiot* I was!" And she hoped he would never know that, when he had asked her, as Mary's nearest friend, what his chances were, she had been so ridiculous as to suppose that he was asking about his chances with herself.

"Don't blame yourself," David said with a laugh. "Mary's very good at concealing her feelings. I wouldn't have given much for my chances myself two hours ago."

"I like that!" declared Mary with amused candour. "*You* concealed your feelings so well that I didn't know whether it was Jess or Angela Onderley that you were after."

"Oh, Mary!" David laughed and pulled a face. "I don't mind your thinking I could fall in love with Jess. Anyone could." And he gave Jessica an affectionate smile, which was entirely devoid of distress or self-consciousness. "But you do my taste less than justice if you think I could fall for Angela. Though I suppose it's very ungallant of me to say so," he added reflectively.

"No, it isn't," declared Jessica with considerable energy. For the mention of Angela made her recall, with something like fury, that it was she who was entirely responsible for starting the ridiculous misapprehension.

That Angela might honestly have made some wrong guesses was understandable. But that she should have stated categorically that David confessed frankly to a passion for Jessica could be nothing less than a plain lie.

"Detestable girl!" thought Jessica with quite unusual heat. "No doubt she saw David had a sort of affectionate, friendly concern for me, and she decided to work that up into something else. I expect she told him, in his turn, that I should probably be forced to marry her brother in order to keep a roof over the children's heads! That would account for his more than friendly worry when I announced my engagement to Ford."

The more Jessica thought about it, the more certain she became that she had hit on the explanation for the series of misunderstandings, and it was all she could do to keep herself from asking David point-blank if Angela had made any such suggestion to him.

However, realising that the less other people knew about Angela's scheming, the less damage there would be done, she managed to contain herself, and joined with sincerity in the congratulations and discussions which naturally followed.

It seemed that neither Mary nor David thought there was any need for a long engagement.

"I dare say we shall be married about the same time as you, Jess," Mary said.

"How *lovely*," Judy exclaimed. "Won't Mrs. Forrest be pleased? She likes weddings."

No one felt able to testify conscientiously to Mrs. Forrest's probable pleasure, since all felt that she had never really intended David to marry at all. So there was a short and noncommittal silence, and then Mary said:

"I like your frock, Jess. It's new, isn't it?"

"Um-hm. There's a three-quarter length coat that goes with it. Come on upstairs and I'll show you," Jessica said, seizing the opportunity for a few minutes alone with her friend. "You can have ten more minutes, children, with David, and then it's definitely bed," she added over her shoulder as she and Mary went out of the room.

The moment they were alone together, Jessica flung her arm round Mary and hugged her.

"Are you frightfully happy, darling?"

"Yes. And frightfully relieved," Mary admitted with candour, and they both laughed.

"Didn't you *really* guess that David was keen?" Jessica enquired, curious to find whether others had been as far out as she in their guesses.

"Well, yes. At least, sometimes I felt nearly sure. But the fact was, of course, that David didn't intend to have anything too obvious until his mother was out of the way," Mary explained frankly. "There's no good in pretending she won't be pretty mad, poor pet, though, of course, she'll get used to the idea, and she likes me personally."

"I'm sure she does," interrupted Jessica warmly.

"But she would have nipped things in the bud if it had struck her there was any bud to nip," Mary retorted shrewdly, but without rancour. "And I don't think David meant to have any trouble of that sort. He's extraordinarily determined, for all his sweet nature, you know."

"So while he was busy hiding things from his mother, he also succeeded in hiding them, to a certain extent, from you?" suggested Jessica amusedly.

"Something like that," Mary agreed. "And then he was so anxious and concerned over you that—I know you'll think this ridiculous, Jess—there *was* a time when I wondered if it were you he was keen on."

"I don't think it's ridiculous at all," Jessica said with some humour. "The same idea struck me, as a matter of fact," and she laughed heartily, because it was such a relief to be able to be frank with Mary about this.

"No. Did it really?" Mary laughed, too, but with a shade of worry in her tone. Then, after a minute she said, "Tell me frankly, Jess—there isn't—I mean—you aren't the least bit disappointed about—about David and me, are you?"

"Not the very least bit in the world, darling!" Jessica assured her with amused emphasis. "I think David's a darling, and I can't imagine anything nicer than you two marrying. I can tell you—I was a good deal upset when it did pass through my mind that he was keen on me, and I'm inexpressibly delighted that it should have been you."

"That's all right, then," Mary said, with a relieved smile.

"Though I'm flattered to think," Jessica added mischievously, "that David should have been so kindly concerned about my illness that we both thought he was in love with me."

Mary laughed, bit her lip, and then said a little doubtfully:

"It wasn't only about your illness that he was worried, you know."

"No?" Jessica raised her eyebrows. "About what else?"

"About your marriage, Jess. And he still is—and so am I."

"You have no need to be," Jessica said slowly, almost coldly. But Mary cut quickly across her denial:

"I hope that's true, but I'm not quite sure. There's something that has to be said, Jess, which must seem not at all my business, and yet"—Mary frowned—"I've got to say it. I can't help knowing—we both can't help knowing—that, except for Ford Onderley's proposal of marriage, you and the twins would have had to accept the sort of life with your uncle and aunt which you would all have hated. I can't get it out of my mind that you may be marrying a man you don't care about. simply to provide a happy home for the children."

"You needn't worry about that," Jessica interrupted, leaning back against the end of her bed and speaking quite steadily. "It just isn't true."

"Well, of course you'd have to say that," Mary said. "I should do just the same myself. And it's nobody's business but your own whether it is the truth or not. But what I want to do—what David and I both want to do—is to remove that sense of compulsion from you, so that you can make a perfectly free choice, Jess."

There was silence in the room for a moment. Then Jessica said, rather uncertainly:

"I don't quite understand."

"No. That's what I wanted to explain," Mary said. "You see, whether you marry Ford Onderley or not, you'll be leaving The Mead soon, won't you?"

Jessica nodded.

"David and I haven't quite worked things out yet, but—we think we'd probably like to make our home here when we get married. It's near Father, it's a place we both know and love and it would suit us in nearly every way. What I want to make clear is that, if you didn't marry and had to have a job instead, David and I would like the twins to stay on in their own home and——"

"Mary!"

Jessica turned quite pale, staggered by the generosity of the offer, well though she knew her friend's warm and impulsive heart.

"Now, don't start exclaiming and objecting," Mary interrupted quickly. "You know I couldn't be fonder of Tom and Judy if they were my own brother and sister, and David thinks they're grand kids too. I know some people would think it odd, starting married life with a couple of kids nearly in their teens, but we don't feel that way at all. They just seem part of The Mead, anyway. And you wouldn't have to get a job so very far away, and could see them at week-ends and that sort of thing. It's not a bad idea, you know."

"It's the most fantastically generous idea I ever heard," Jessica said in a rather low voice.

"But one which anyone might accept from such an old friend as I am," Mary pointed out. "That is"—she paused—"if you want to accept it. There's no need for you to say anything right away, pet. Just think it over. But I want you to have it firmly fixed in your mind that there is no reason—no reason at all—for you to marry *anyone* unless you love him. Now show me that coat."

Dazedly, Jessica went over to the wardrobe and, more by chance than design, lifted out the right garment.

She knew she had not expressed her thanks to Mary. She knew she had not said any of the dozen phrases of gratitude and astonishment which crowded into her mind. But, if she said much, she thought she would cry. And then Mary would be quite sure she was weeping with relief.

"I'll explain to her afterwards," Jessica thought almost incoherently. "I'll tell her that no one ever, ever had such a wonderfully generous and understanding friend. No one but Mary—and David—would have thought of such a thing! It isn't that I want an escape— at least, do I? But to know that I can make my own decision, without being torn this way and that by the thought of the happiness or distress of the children —that's something I'd never dared to hope for."

"It's a sweet coat," Mary was saying with genuine admiration.

"Yes, isn't it?" murmured Jessica absently. Then suddenly she tossed the coat down on to the bed and flung her arms round her friend. "Oh, Mary, I do love you very much!" she exclaimed.

And Mary laughed and hugged her very tightly in return, and quite obviously understood all the things which Jessica had wanted to say, but which would probably remain for ever unsaid.

"All right. I know," Mary said comprehensively.

And then the twins came rushing upstairs to bed, and Mary said it was time that she and David were going.

Jessica strolled as far as the gate with them when they went, and, after she had waved them goodbye, she walked idly round the garden, pinching off an occasional dead blossom or stooping to pull up a weed, but without much real consciousness of what she was doing.

The only thing of which she was acutely conscious was the warm, familiar hush of her own garden on a late summer's evening. It had been a hot day, and, as the light faded and the brilliant colours of daylight began to fade into the delicate monochrome of evening, a faint breeze drifted over the garden, reviving the drooping flowers and plants and drawing an intensified fragrance from them.

"How lovely it is," thought Jessica. "How lovely and peaceful it is—and I'm free! At least—what was it that Mary had said? That there was no reason for me to marry *anyone,* unless I loved him."

She stood on the smooth green lawn, looking away across the country towards Oaklands. She need never go there as Ford's wife—unless she loved him. Shorn of all the secondary considerations, the harrowing attendant responsibilities, her decision could be made, simply and clearly, on the basis of what she really wished.

With a sensation as though a physical weight rolled from her shoulders, Jessica stretched out her arms with a little laugh of happiness and relief.

And, in that moment of freedom and clear vision,

she knew suddenly and inevitably that Ford was the man she wanted.

Not as the sarcastically indulgent landlord, not as the kind and protective person who would stand between her and the ever-growing financial troubles, not even as the universal provider for herself and the twins. But, quite simply, as the man she had, almost unknowingly, grown to love.

"I never saw him quite clearly until this moment," Jessica thought. "I always *had* to see him in some special light or another, because I needed him. It isn't like that any longer! I don't *have* to marry him. I just want to marry him."

She was so enchanted and excited by the discovery that she felt she could have run all the way to Oaklands now, to tell him of it.

But, apart from the absurdity of arriving there a second time in one evening for no better reason than that she wished to tell him that she loved him, Jessica realised, with something of a disagreeable shock, that she was not really at all sure how Ford would take such a declaration.

That he was fond of her she knew. That he wanted—indeed, had been quite determined—to marry her she also knew. But declarations of passionate love had not entered into their relationship at all.

Slowly Jessica retraced her steps across the lawn.

If Angela's statements were to be trusted though, of course, they were not, thought Jessica, angrily recalling the lie about David—Ford's affection for herself was of a very temperate and well-balanced variety, and he would be more likely to be disconcerted than enraptured by any romantic confession of hers.

"Not that one can go by what Angela says," Jessica assured herself impatiently. "She's quite capable of telling me a lot of poppycock about Ford, just as she did about David. She simply arranges facts to suit her own purpose."

But she had definitely thought it worth while to bring Paula into Ford's vicinity again. And Ford had looked as near put out as she had ever seen him, at the prospect of Paula's coming to Oaklands.

"There's *something* in it," Jessica reluctantly admitted. "Even if it's not quite what Angela wants to make out."

And she wished very much that Paula's visit were over, or that she could have some tangible proof that Ford no longer cared for the glamorous original of that photograph in Angela's room.

But, in spite of her anxiety and the first stirrings of jealousy which she had ever experienced, Jessica could not help feeling excited and happy as she lay in bed that night, watching the long streak of moonlight from the window travel slowly across the carpet.

She loved Ford and she was going to marry him, and surely—surely every other consideration faded into insignificance beside that?

The next day happened to be a busy one for Jessica, and, presumably, for Ford too, because by teatime he had still not put in an appearance. Inexplicably, she felt in a mood of nervous expectancy, as though at any moment she might receive some significant news— either good or bad. And, when Judy dashed into tea and cried dramatically, "Guess what!" Jessica felt her heart give an uncomfortable lurch.

"What has happened?" she asked, rather breathlessly.

"You'll never believe it," declared Judy, prolonging the agony unnecessarily. "But that extraordinary geometry answer was right, and I got full marks, and I was the *only one* in the class that did. Fortunately, Miss Dobson didn't ask me to explain how I got it, because I couldn't possibly have done it again. It was just a fluke the first time. Still, it was a nice fluke, wasn't it?"

Jessica said it was, and knew it was mean and unreasonable of her to feel so profoundly irritated as her little sister babbled on about the interesting reactions of Miss Dobson and the rest of the class.

But later on she decided, just as she had the previous evening, that she would go over to Oaklands herself. She felt she must see him—look at him with her newly opened eyes—judge for herself what his real reaction to her might be. Perhaps if she called him "darling" again. . . . He had been genuinely pleased and moved when she had done so before.

But that had slipped out quite naturally. Now she understood why. She couldn't deliberately arrange to call him "darling" in advance. That wouldn't be the same thing at all. But, anyway, she must see him.

It was a Friday—that blessed evening when home-work can be safely shelved until the next day—and so the twins were rolling the lawn, and only paused to wave to her as she left the house.

She hoped that this time too she would meet Ford before she reached Oaklands. But she arrived at the house without having seen anything of him, and, to her chagrin, when the servant ushered her into the lounge, only Angela was sitting there.

"Hallo, Jessica." Angela sounded quite affable. "Did you drop in to see Ford?"

"Yes." Jessica hoped she sounded just as affable in her turn. "But it looks as though I must have missed him on the way."

"Oh, no," Angela explained easily. "He's somewhere about the grounds with Paula. You know, my friend, Paula Dryden. She's come here to stay for a while."

Jessica controlled the angry impulse to ask why *she* was not running around the grounds with her friend Paula Dryden, and said as casually as possibly, "Then I'll wait."

She sat down, finding, to her dismay and annoyance, that she was trembling slightly.

Paula had certainly not wasted any time in answering the telegraphed invitation! And now here she was, firmly established at Oaklands—the romantic subject of a broken engagement, with something of a claim on Ford's sympathetic attention, if only for the sake of old friendship.

There could not have been a situation which she would have detested more heartily, Jessica thought angrily. But, because it was important that Angela should not guess how deeply depressed she was by it, it was necessary to make some sort of effort at bright conversation. And, more with the idea of hiding her own discomfort than of creating it in Angela, she said:

"I suppose David has told you about his engage-ment?"

"Yes, I must say I was surprised."

"You must have been, considering your own theory," replied Jessica dryly, and with what she felt to be excusable irony.

Angela laughed, but looked quite unabashed.

"Oh, I didn't mean only because of that," she said. "I'm surprised that anyone as 'fly' as David should be caught by Mary Skelton. But, of course, she meant to have him."

Jessica felt the furious colour rush into her face.

"Mary happens to be my best friend," she reminded Angela curtly, "and I certainly won't sit here and hear anyone speak of her like that. There was never any question of her trying to 'catch' him. David is very much in love with Mary, and they are obviously as happy and well suited as it's possible to be."

"Very generous of you," murmured Angela with a slight and altogether infuriating smile.

"It's not generous. It's just a statement of fact," Jessica retorted sharply. "And, of course, I'm very happy about it because I happen to be extremely fond of them both." And then, as her anger got the better of her: "I'm afraid the trouble with you, Angela, is that you just don't *like* other people to be happy. You'd rather have things go wrong than see them work out happily and pleasantly."

Angela raised her eyebrows, but more in protest at Jessica's indecent candour than anything else.

"And I'm afraid that you really don't like me at all, Jessica," she said mockingly.

"No," Jessica said slowly. "I think you're detestable."

And then she felt very much ashamed of herself, and added quickly, "I—I'm sorry. I shouldn't have said that."

"'s a little difficult to take back," Angela remarked dryly.

.is was so true that Jessica was dismayedly silent.

She could, of course, have told Angela just why she thought her detestable—upbraided her for having deliberately tried to make trouble over David, told her she suspected her of trying to use Paula's presence for further trouble.

162

But suddenly it all seemed very trivial and undignified. And she wished quite passionately that she had not allowed herself to be betrayed into such an unequivocal statement of feeling.

After a moment she got up.

"I think I'll go and find Ford," she said rather stiffly.

"As you like."

Angela's air indicated that she could not have cared less *what* Jessica did with herself. And, feeling oddly shaken by the disagreeable encounter, Jessica went out of the room.

As she reached the door, Angela called after her:

"You'll probably find them round about the garage. Ford took Paula to see your car."

Another spasm of indignation assailed Jessica. Why on earth did Ford want to take the girl to see *her* car? It was something between her and Ford. Nothing to do with Paula. Why couldn't he have shown her the grounds, or the view, or something equally innocuous?

"Don't be silly," Jessica admonished herself. "You're just looking for trouble. Probably Angela mentioned the car, and Paula said she'd like to see it. He could not do less than show it to her then, could he?"

With this thought determinedly in mind, she crossed the wide yard to the garage, noticing, as she did so, that the big sliding door was partially pushed back, which suggested that there was someone in there.

Instinctively, she braced herself almost physically for this first encounter with Paula Dryden, pausing for a second in the doorway as she did so.

Then, at the sight which met her eyes, she stepped back again immediately, so that the corner of the garage concealed her. She had had only a second's glimpse of what was happening in the garage, but that second was sufficient.

Ford and Paula were not standing there casually admiring the car. Paula—slim and appealing in a glamorous red suit—had her arms round Ford's neck and her face half hidden against him. And, in that one moment, Jessica had seen that he had his arms round her.

CHAPTER ELEVEN

VERY quietly Jessica withdrew from the spot where she had been standing and, rather blindly, made her way towards the wicket gate which led from the grounds of Oaklands into the wood.

If the encounter with Angela had left her shaken, the sight which she had just witnessed left her feeling sick and cold.

"It's not true!" she murmured to herself, in a sort of angry dismay. "I don't believe it! I—I ought to have looked more thoroughly and made sure."

But—made sure of what? Of what was she in doubt? One glance had been quite sufficient to identify the two figures and establish the fact that they were in each other's arms. What more did she want?

This was not something which Angela had arranged. At least—she had provided the setting, of course, and arranged the dangerous propinquity which was to batter down all Ford's recently built defences. But the situation would have been harmless if he had not really cared.

Jessica opened the wicket gate, passed through, and closed it carefully after her, taking time about all her actions, as though she were performing something of importance which might conceivably distract her attention from her maddening thoughts.

Then she left the path which would have taken her straight back home, and plunged into the green, shaded byways of the wood, where she could feel alone. She did not want to go home. She did not want to go back to Oaklands. Not ever, she felt at that moment.

All she wanted was to get away by herself. Only that was no escape from her thoughts.

"It's partly my own fault," she thought painfully. "I've held him so lightly, shirked any statement that I loved him. But I didn't know until yesterday!"

Suppose she had been able to tell him in the beginning that she loved him—that she found him thrilling and amusing and dear and wonderful? Would they not have built something lovely and substantial between them, which would have withstood any petty onslaughts of a mere Paula?

But there had never been anything like that. He had been kind and indulgent, and she had been grateful and conscientious. What sort of basis was that for a romance? How could that compare with the passionate wave of emotion with which Paula no doubt had enveloped him?

And, at the thought of Paula hanging round his neck, Jessica experienced a hot, blind wave of jealousy which was the most primitive feeling she had ever known. It left her scared and shocked. As though some protective, civilised veneer had been stripped from her and left her rough and crude and elemental.

"I hate Paula," Jessica thought starkly. "I could kill her." And though she murmured aloud, "Don't be silly," she knew that that impulse had risen from the very core of her being.

But *he* didn't hate Paula. He loved her still, it seemed. And, that being so, what must he be thinking now of the horrible predicament in which he had placed himself?

Engaged to one girl and tied to her by every claim which need could make on a generous nature—and yet loving someone else.

"That is, if he does really love her," thought Jessica, snatching for a moment at a straw of hope. "Perhaps it's just infatuation."

But no momentary infatuation would cover the facts. No one denied that Ford and Paula had known each other for years, and he had undoubtedly been put out at the thought of her coming to Oaklands. Angela might have lied shamelessly about David, but Jessica was afraid that her statements about Ford and Paula were substantially correct.

And there was nothing *he* could do about it. He had committed himself to the task of providing a home and future, not only for the girl to whom he was engaged, but for two entirely dependent children, too. There was their future to be considered, apart from the three actors in the "triangle" drama themselves. Unless . . .

With a sensation of something like superstitious awe, Jessica suddenly recalled Mary's offer of the previous evening.

"It's as though it were in preparation for this horrible discovery," thought Jessica dazedly. And presently she sat down on the grass, to try to work out the situation calmly.

At first, her mind instinctively rejected any solution of the problem which involved her giving up Ford. But, almost immediately, she forced herself to admit that she had no right to try to keep him, if the girl he really wanted was now free.

"It's I who must step down," she told herself determinedly. "All the more so because it was on a generous and quixotic impulse that he saddled himself with the responsibility of the twins and myself. At least, I suppose it was."

She buried her face in her hands, and tried to recall exactly how he had looked and sounded when he asked her to marry him. But the effort brought him so clearly before her, with such a painful realisation of all she was losing, that she hastily abandoned the attempt, and tried to think instead of Mary's offer.

That had been made, of course, with the original intention of saving her from a marriage which Mary and David thought she did not want. Well, she *didn't* want it, unless it would mean happiness for Ford as well as herself.

If the future happiness of the twins could be secured by their remaining at The Mead with Mary, then there was no reason at all why she should not take a job and earn her own living, leaving Ford free to marry Paula.

It was the decent and simple way out of the tangle.

"But I don't want to lose him," Jessica said aloud. "I don't want to lose him. Why didn't I understand before that I was supremely lucky and happy in having him? Though, of course, this means that I never really did have him," she reminded herself sadly—without, however, entirely convincing herself of the fact.

Anyway, what did it matter now? She would have to let him go. After what she had just seen, she could never hold him to his bond and be happy. The best thing would be to go and see Mary right away and tell her that her offer was going to be accepted.

Reluctantly, Jessica dragged herself to her feet and started off towards the Skeltons' house.

Severel times on the way she hesitated, as though half-deciding not to commit herself quite so far on the impulse of the moment. And yet, if she did not do it now, she was not sure that she would be able to do it at all.

When she came in sight of Mary's house, she saw, to her relief, that her friend was in the garden alone. So at least she would not have to make the effort of knocking on the door and enquiring for her, and probably become involved in conversation with Mr. Skelton.

Mary looked up at the sound of the gate-latch, and came towards her immediately.

"Hell, Jess. I'm so glad you came over. I'm feeling rather flat because Daddy and David have gone over to Keswick on some sort of business and haven't come back yet."

Jessica murmured something noncommital, and took the garden chair which Mary pushed forward.

"Well, what's the news?"

Mary was smiling, with the happy expectancy of the person who is so pleased with life that she cannot anticipate anything but good news.

Jessica didn't answer at once. She was groping for some sort of phrase which might lead up to what she wanted to say, and not make the whole thing sound so bald and crude. But her mind refused to supply her with the words she wanted, and after a few minutes she said in a low voice:

"The news is that I want to accept the offer which you made last night."

Mary caught her breath, and the smile faded from her face.

She was not entirely surprised to receive this statement. Only, somehow, she had not expected it to be accompanied by the indefinable suggestion of tragedy. After all, if Jess wished to accept the offer, it must mean that she saw in it a means of escape from something she dreaded, and that was surely a cause for relief, rather than dismay.

"I'm—glad," she said doubtfully at last. "At least, I mean I'm glad that you feel willing to trust the twins to David and me. And I'm glad if our offer enables you to—to escape from a marriage which you don't feel would have turned out well."

"No," Jessica said slowly. "I don't think Ford and I should be happy—married to each other."

Mary was silent. She felt sure there was something here which she did not understand, but hesitated to enquire further. Finally, she said rather diffidently:

"Does Ford—know yet?"

"No."

Mary wished Jessica would not look so pale and harassed. It made her wonder if she were afraid to tell Ford of her decision.

"He wouldn't want to hold you to the engagement if he knew you didn't really want it."

"No. Oh, no—he won't want to hold me to the engagement," Jessica agreed, with a queer little laugh which had no amusement in it.

Mary glanced at her sharply.

"Why do you say it like that, Jess?"

"Oh, I don't know." Jessica pushed back her hair from her forehead, as though she found it too heavy. Then she met Mary's worried glance, and, with an effort, she pulled herself together and smiled. "It's all right, Mary. I don't much like the idea of having to tell him, and—and it's upsetting to have to take a decision like this and rearrange everything."

This sounded plausible enough. But Mary seemed curiously unconvinced. She looked at her friend for a moment with slightly widened eyes. Then, as though the words surprised even herself, she said:

"Look here, Jess. I suppose you're quite sure you *don't* want to marry him?"

Jessica looked away. She thought of the girl she had seen in Ford's arms, and how she really belonged to his world and his life, how she had known him for years, and obviously had been in no doubt about expressing *her* feelings for him. And, after a pause which Mary found long enough to be disturbing, she said:

"Quite sure."

Mary bit her lip.

"Then there's no more to be said, dear. Except that of course David and I will be delighted to have the twins at The Mead quite indefinitely. You don't have to worry about them at all. When your—your luck changes and you find you can have them with you again, you only have to say so. Until then, their home is with us."

Jessica made a little gesture, expressive of her gratitude, and Mary caught her outstretched hand and held it. Neither of them said anything for a moment. Then Jessica stood up and said, in a small but determined voice:

"I'll go and tell Ford now."

Mary knew that too much expressed sympathy would probably be unnerving, rather than consoling, at this moment. So she just went with Jessica to the gate and waved to her.

She didn't like to comment on the fact that Jessica started off in the direction of her home, and not towards Oaklands at all.

But Jessica was not too dazed not to know what she was doing. And one thing she was determined upon—that she would not set foot in Oaklands again. Ford would be sure to come to The Mead some time that evening—unless he were too much agitated by the scene with Paula—and she would do her explaining then.

As a matter of fact, she had not even so long to wait as that. He overtook her—driving in the lovely little new car which was to have been hers—before she reached the gate of The Mead.

"Hallo, Jess!"

He drew to a standstill beside her, and greeted her with a smiling gaiety which she found rather grimly courageous of him, in the circumstances. Evidently he meant to go through with his bargain, with a good grace.

"Hallo."

She gave him the best smile she could manage, in her turn.

"Jump in. I was just driving your car up to the house."

Jessica felt her throat tighten. She could not possibly let him drive the car up to The Mead, have the twins receive it with rapturous enthusiasm, and then explain that, in the circumstances, he must take it back again.

He must have seen the hesitation on her face, because he smiled, as he leant forward to open the door for her, and said:

"What's the matter? Don't you trust my driving yet?"

"Yes, of course. It—it's not that."

She got in beside him. Then, just as he was about to start the car again, she said:

"Don't drive straight to The Mead, Ford. I—let's drive around a bit. I want to talk to you."

"Just as you like. Where shall we go?" He started the car.

"Anywhere. It—doesn't matter."

He glanced at her.

"Well, it's your car," he said, lightly. "You ought to decide where it should go."

"No. At least—that's just it, Ford. It isn't my car. I mean—I can't accept it."

"Good lord, why ever not?"

"Well, you see"—she gripped her hands together—"Ford, I'm sorry, but I'm not going to marry you after all."

For a moment after she had said that she dared not look at him. There was no immediate and dramatic response. No exclamations or protestations, no abrupt slackening or increasing of the car's speed. Then, after a short silence, he said:

"When did you come to this decision?"

Jessica made some rapid calculations, in view of the fact that she would have to give some plausible story.

"I—I've been thinking about it for some time. I finally decided last night."

"Last night! But I thought——" He stopped, and

170

then said, "Never mind. What are your plans for the future then, Jess? For you—and the twins, I mean?"

She did glance at him then, and saw that, though he was perfectly calm, he was a little pale and his eyes glittered rather curiously. She wondered how much frantic relief and hope that set expression hid.

He must be wondering how much he dared to believe his luck, and whether he ought to make some sort of protest, for decency's sake.

But she didn't want to hear him make meaningless protests. She didn't want him to be forced into pretending dismay, in order to save *her* face. And she knew in that moment that she must take on herself the full onus of breaking the engagement.

"It's because the twins' future has been assured that I—that I can take this decision," she explained, a little breathlessly. "You know that Mary is going to marry David Forrest?"

He nodded briefly.

"Well, they want to start their married life at The Mead, and they—they're perfectly willing to give the twins a home there with them."

"But I was perfectly willing to give the twins a home with us at Oaklands," he said rather harshly.

"I know, I know. You've been wonderfully generous, but——"

"For heaven's sake don't call me generous again," he said almost savagely. And she bit her lip and was silent, understanding very well that he must hate to have his generosity stressed, and the role of injured party thrust upon him, when what she was saying must be the best news he had heard for a long time.

He seemed to realise, after a moment, how violently he had spoken, because he said, in a much quieter tone:

"I'm sorry. Please go on. About Mary and David Forrest wanting to take the twins, I mean."

"Well, that—that's all."

"You mean that you thankfully jumped at the offer?"

She felt herself go pale.

"Ford"—she spoke with an effort—"you said once before that you—you realised that for me the most important thing in the world was to provide for the future happiness of Judy and Tom. I didn't quite admit it at the time, but I didn't deny it. And, of course, it—it was true."

"You mean that was the only real hold I had on you?"

She was silent, thinking dismayedly of the terrible, unconfessed hold he had on her, and always would have now.

He waited, presumably expecting her to speak. Then, when the lengthened silence had answered for her, he said quietly:

"Then the fact is that, free of the necessity of providing a home for the twins, you definitely don't want to marry me. Is that it?"

This was the moment, of course, when she must put her decision into a categorical statement.

Jessica had thought she was prepared for it, and was proof against the misery of the actual moment of renunciation. But she would never have believed that pronouncing a few words could hurt so much. To her surprise, she found that her heart literally ached with the effort.

But the effort had to be made. All the rest was pointless unless she could achieve this final victory over herself. And, in a small, but perfectly firm voice, she said:

"Yes, that's it. I—I definitely don't want to marry you."

In her determination to be plain, she was afraid she had achieved a degree of ungraciousness too. And that seemed to be more or less his view. Because his tone was curt as he said:

"Then there's no more to say about it. Shall I drive you home now?"

"Yes, please," Jessica said, and wished she were dead.

They drove back in silence—Jessica too exhausted to say anything more, and Ford presumably finding silence the best refuge from the problem of balancing inward relief against the necessity for an outward appearance of chagrin.

Only as they neared the gate of The Mead did Jessica rouse herself to say:

"Ford, I don't want you to think I was only concerned with making a convenience of you because of the twins."

"I don't think that." He smiled grimly, but didn't look at her.

"I—I do tremendously appreciate all the kindness and thought, you know. It's just——"

"All right. I understand."

"And I'm sorry I ran you into all that extra expense for the car."

"It doesn't matter," he told her. And she wondered if he were thinking that it would do for Paula instead.

The thought was so unpalatable that she thrust it from her. And, as he drew up outside the gate, she took her engagement ring off her finger, with what seemed to her a physical wrench.

"You—you'd better have this." She held it out to him.

For a moment he looked at it as though he hardly recognised it. Then, with a quick movement, he closed her outstretched hand on the ring again.

"No, no. You keep that." He sounded as nearly agitated as she had ever heard him.

"But I can't, Ford. One—one always gives back the ring at the end of a—of a broken engagement."

"I don't care what 'one' always does. Please keep your ring. I want you to."

And, taking her hand, he put the ring back on her finger.

Jessica stared down at her hand, wondering if he realised that, in his agitation, he had thrust the ring back on her "engagement" finger. She supposed she ought to say that at any rate she would have to wear it on another finger. But instead she only murmured distressedly:

"Why do you want me to keep it?"

"Because I'd like you to have something of mine," he said curtly.

And she thought then that perhaps he felt less in her debt that way. As though the ring were a silent thank-offering for having been painlessly released from his engagement.

"Very well," Jessica said slowly. "I'll keep it. Thank you, Ford."

And then she got out of the car and said good night to him.

It was impossible to kiss him, of course, and it seemed equally impossible to shake hands with the man one loved. So she just stood there with her hands behind her back as she said good night.

Neither of them actually said goodbye. But, as he drove away, in the little car that was to have been hers, she knew that he was driving out of her life.

As she walked slowly through the garden to the house, she recalled, with unbearable poignancy, her rapturous discovery of the previous evening.

Was it really only yesterday that she had known so certainly and so finally that she loved Ford and that she was to marry him and be so happy?

Everything had seemed so secure and inevitable then. For a few brief hours she had actually known the fairy-tale sweetness of the "happy ever after" feeling.

And now all that was over.

She had released him of her own free will. For that was the quaint term one used to describe the agonising kind of renunciation which she had just staged. Of her own free will, she had left him free to marry Paula, instead of herself. Paula, who, if she were at all like her friend Angela, would simply think her a perfect fool to have made such a gesture.

For a moment, Jessica wondered, in a sort of sick panic, why she *had* made the gesture. Why, without careful thought and consideration, she had sacrificed the thing she wanted most in the world.

It was a quixotic impulse, of course. Like the quixotic impulse which had moved him to ask her to marry him, because he liked her and was sorry for her desperate plight.

Perhaps, thought Jessica, with a faint smile, it was poetic justice that he should have entangled himself in an engagement for a generous impulse, and been released on the strength of another.

But there was not much to make Jessica smile that evening, and, as she went into the house, she felt her heart sink almost literally at the thought of the terrible change in her hopes and plans which had taken place since she went out.

"Jess! Je-ess, is that you?" called Judy from upstairs.

"Good gracious, aren't you in bed yet?" Jessica responded mechanically.

"Oh, yes. I'm in bed. But I want you to come up and speak to me."

With what, Jessica supposed, Angela would have considered "indulgence," she went upstairs and into Judy's room. Her little sister popped up from under the bed-clothes in some excitement.

"Was that the sound of the car bringing you home? I thought I heard it stop at the gate?"

"Yes. Ford drove me home."

"In the new car?"

"Y-yes. In the new car."

"But it drove *away* again, Jess. I thought Ford was going to leave it here." Judy was palpably disappointed.

Jessica sat down rather wearily on the end of the bed, feeling quite beyond inventing explanations by now, and aware that she must somehow stem Judy's rising pleasure in the car, unless there was to be a proportionate state of woe when she discovered there was not to be a car after all.

"Judy dear, don't get in quite such a state about the car," she began desperately. "It's not—I mean, I don't think I'm going to have it after all."

"Not have it?" Judy spoke in shocked capitals. "Do you mean Ford doesn't mean to give it you as a present? Was it a mistake?"

"N-not exactly."

"How do you mean—not exactly?" enquired the exact Judy, who liked things to be perfectly clear.

"Judy, it—it's quite the wrong time of night to start explanations, and I don't know that I can give you much of an explanation, anyway. But I'm not letting Ford give me the car, because I—I'm not going to marry him after all. You'll have to know quite soon, so you may as well know now, I suppose."

Judy's mouth literally fell open. Then, because she could never resist giving a hand when she thought a situation required it, she said briskly:

"Couldn't you make it up, perhaps?"

"Make it up? Oh, we haven't quarrelled. We've just decided—I really can't explain."

"Aren't we going to live at Oaklands after all, then?" This frightful aspect of the case had only just struck Judy.

"I'm afraid not."

"You—you don't mean it's boarding school and Uncle Hector and Aunt Miriam, after all?"

"No, no. Don't look so scared. You'll like the new arrangement tremendously," Jessica assured her hastily. "Mary and David are going to live here, and you're going to live here with them."

Judy brightened momentarily. But sudden suspicion darkened her world again.

"And Tom too?"

"Oh, yes. Tom will be here too."

"And you?"

"Well, I shall be here for week-ends and holidays and——"

"What holidays?" Judy wanted to know suspiciously.

"Well, you see, I shall have to get some sort of a job and earn my own living. Then I'll make lots of money and start saving up for when I can make a home with you two again," Jessica explained with false brightness.

"That means you won't be here very often."

"Fairly often," Jessica said—unconvincingly, she felt.

"But you won't be *living* here."

"Not exactly. But——"

"Oh, I don't like the idea at all," cried Judy. "It's nothing like as nice as having us all live at Oaklands."

"But, Judy, you love Mary and David."

"Yes. But I love you better," Judy retorted. "And, anyway, I love Ford too. Oh, it's a much better idea for us all to live together at Oaklands. Then we can come and see Mary and David whenever we like, but you'll be always there. Oh, Jess, do make it up with him!" For Judy still seemed unable to accept any explanation for the cancelled engagement which did not include a mendable quarrel.

"We haven't quarrelled, I tell you. There's nothing *to* make up," Jessica repeated desperately, feeling that it was an unnecessary refinement of cruelty which forced her to argue against the very thing she most wanted.

"Well, then, I don't see what the trouble is," Judy cried. "Oh, Jess, think how lovely it would be at Oaklands. Ford is so kind and such fun. And when Angela's gone it would be perfect. Don't you *want* to live there?"

"Oh, Judy, stop it!" exclaimed Jessica. And, to the great dismay of both of them, she suddenly began to cry.

"Jess!" Judy knelt up in bed, appalled by this unusual sight, and flung her arms round her sister. "Don't cry! Oh, how awful. Why are you crying? Has he said he doesn't want to marry you?"

"No, no. It's nothing like that. I'm just being silly."

"Have you said you don't want him, and now you're sorry?"

"No." Jessica shook her head, and rejected this accurate statement of the case with vehemence.

"But it must be something. Is it that you're disappointed about losing the car?"

And, because she had to give some reason and Judy seemed to think this ridiculous explanation quite a possible one, Jessica nodded and said:

"Yes. It's that more than anything. I always wanted a car. But it can't be helped now, and I've got over it." She dried her eyes, and tried to look as though the loss of a car could really produce this devastating state of affairs.

Judy regarded her doubtfully.

"Are you sure it's all right now?"

"Yes. Quite sure. I was just tired and disappointed. I'll be all right in the morning. And—and don't worry about the future. We'll manage to have good times here, as we always have."

This general promise of brighter things seemed to quiet some of Judy's doubts, and presently she lay down and allowed Jessica to tuck her in.

"P'raps you'll be able to get a job quite near, and

then you could live here, too," she suggested hopefully.

And Jessica allowed herself the weakness of saying, "Perhaps I could," because it was quite impossible to explain to Judy at the moment that no young couple— not even the understanding Mary and David—would wish to add a grownup and two children to their early marriage ménage.

Judy, however, was greatly consoled by this inspiration of hers, and was already viewing the altered future with cheerful resignation when Jessica said good night to her and finally left her.

But for Jessica there was no mood of cheerful resignation. Somehow, the conversation with Judy had served only to emphasize the blankness and emptiness of the future.

"Not that I mind standing on my own feet," Jessica told herself earnestly. "And I'm very lucky to have had Mary and David to solve the worst part of my difficulties."

And then she fell to wondering what she would have done if Mary had *not* made such an offer. If the happiness of the twins had been in doubt, would she have refused to accept the implications of that scene between Ford and Paula? If Oaklands had been the only home available for them, would she have grimly kept Ford to his bargain, and have seen that they made the best of it?

And, if so, what would "the best of it" have been? Might Ford not have resigned himself very well to second-best, and eventually have been very happy with her?

Jessica went to the window of her bedroom, and stood looking out into the darkness, in what she judged to be roughly the direction of Oaklands. And immediately her thoughts flew where her sight could not follow, and she wondered if Ford were at this moment telling Paula that there was no longer any barrier between them.

There would be a decent interval, of course, between the breaking of one engagement and the announcing of the other. But the thing was as good as done. She had resigned him to Paula, and her part in his life was over.

For a long time she stood looking out over the darkened countryside. And then, because one had to go to bed, even if one would not sleep, she slowly drew the curtains, as though to shut out something, and wearily began to undress.

CHAPTER TWELVE

BY breakfast-time next morning, Jessica had braced herself to face the fresh questions which Judy would have thought up in the interval, backed by the slower—but no less searching—enquiries of Tom.

But, to her surprise, neither of them even mentioned the subject of her broken engagement.

It was hard to believe that they had both risen to such heights of tact that they had mutually agreed to say nothing. And Jessica could only think that they had grown so used to threatened upheaval that they were prepared to accept this fresh proposal for the future with stolid calm. That being so, possibly the more urgent problem of getting to school on time presented itself, at the moment, as being of greater importance.

In addition, Judy had lost her history book, and a frantic search took place, to the accompaniment of wails that no one else ever lost their history book and it would be quite impossible to go to school without it. Finally, it was run to earth in improbable seclusion under a cushion in the drawing-room, though Judy was positive that it had never been outside the dining-room. And by then it was time for them both to depart at a brisk trot.

Unnatural quiet seemed to descend on the house when they had gone, and Jessica determinedly set about her household tasks with a concentration which she hoped would keep unhappy thoughts at bay.

The children lunched at school, so she had not the distraction—pleasant or otherwise—of their company in the middle of the day. And, by the middle of the afternoon, she was thinking desperately around her own affairs once more.

With distaste she faced the fact that she would have to write to Uncle Hector and Aunt Miriam with some sort of explanation. For, although she hoped to be able to dispense with their financial help as early as she would have had she married Ford, they were certainly entitled to know something of the new situation.

"But I need not do it this afternoon," Jessica thought, with great reluctance for the task. "There's no hurry for a day or two." And she hoped that, in this, she was displaying well-balanced common sense, rather than sheer cowardice.

Tom came in first, and, even then—though the fact of finding Jessica alone might well have seemed an opportunity for speaking—he still refrained from saying anything.

"It's almost unnatural," thought Jessica, puzzled and amused. "Doesn't he *know* about it? Surely Judy can't have kept it to herself. They always tell each other everything."

But, if Tom had nothing to say, Judy was obviously bursting with information when she came in.

"I'm sorry I'm late. There was something I had to do," she explained, with gratified importance exuding from every pore.

"Had you?" Jessica smiled at her. "Well, come and have your tea now."

"Just a moment," begged Judy, as though the fate of nations hung on the next few moments. "There's something I must say to you, Jess. Come into the drawing-room for a minute, *please.*"

"Is it a secret, then?" Tom wanted to know.

"Yes. But I'll tell you after," Judy promised.

And, a good deal amused, Jessica allowed herself to be led into the drawing-room.

"Well, what is it?" she asked, sitting down and watching Judy shut the door with exaggerated care.

Then Judy rushed across and hugged her.

"It's about the car," she explained. "It's quite all right. You're to have it, after all."

"Have it after all?" gasped Jessica with a funny, empty feeling in the pit of her stomach. "What do you mean?"

"I went to see Ford. That's why I was late."

"Judy!"

"I had the idea last night, after you'd gone. I knew Ford must have wanted you to have the car really, or else why did he buy it? And it seemed silly you should be upsetting yourself about it like that, when he wanted you to have it. I didn't tell Tom," Judy explained, "because I thought he might say it was interfering. But I nearly *burst* with wanting to tell him. Still, I can tell him, now it's all over and——"

"Judy, will you please go back to the bit about your going to see Ford," Jessica interrupted firmly. "What—what did you say to him?"

"Oh, I explained that I knew about the engagement being broken, and I said I knew that was his business and yours," Judy conceded magnanimously. "But I said you'd cried awfully when you got in last night."

"Judy!"

"And that it was because you weren't going to have the car after all, and did he mind awfully if you had it, even if you weren't engaged to him?"

"What did he say?" Jessica asked faintly.

"Do you really want to know what he said?"

"Of course."

"Swear words and all?"

"I suppose so."

"Well, he said, 'Good God! of course she can have it—or anything else she wants. Why the devil didn't she tell me she would like it? Doesn't she know she's welcome to every damned thing I've got?'"

"He said—that?"

"Yes. But he was very upset, I think," Judy explained —in extenuation of his language, presumably.

"I don't understand," Jessica murmured, and put her face in her hands.

"Oh, Jess! It's perfectly simple," cried Judy, exasperated by her sister's apparent denseness. "He said——"

"Yes, I know. I understand that part."

"Anyway, he's driving the car over right away. I think that's him now, so I'll go and have my tea with Tom," Judy finished with an air of tremendous tact.

"Wait a minute."

Judy paused at the door and looked back at her sister.

"No. It's all right." Jessica had just realised that there was nothing to do with this new situation but deal with it on her own, and she waved her young sister away.

Anyway, what had he meant — what had he *meant* by saying that she ought to know she was welcome to everything he had? *That* was not the way a man talked when he wanted to give a girl something as a sop to his conscience.

Like Mary, Ford was used now to walking in and out of the house as he pleased, and he apparently had no thought that a broken engagement might have deprived him of that right, for she heard him come into the hall and say:

"Here, Judy! Where is she?"

"I'm here," Jessica called rather faintly, and he came straight across the hall and into the room, closing the door after him.

Jessica stood up rather uncertainly, and faced him as he leant against the door.

"I—I'm sorry, Ford, that Judy should have come to you and told you all that."

"I'm not," he interrupted curtly. "Why did you cry last night?"

She was used to his coming straight to the point, but the brutal directness of this disconcerted her.

"Judy exaggerated——" she began.

"But you did cry."

"Oh, well—girls cry for lots of things, you know," she protested feebly.

"No, they don't. Not your sort of girl. You hardly ever cry about anything, and you've had plenty to make you cry in the last few months. You weren't really crying because you wanted the car, were you?"

"N-no. Of course not."

"Why, then?" He crossed the room suddenly and had her in his arms. "Jess, what are you *doing* to us both? Why won't you let us take the happiness that's there? Is it because you resent having me supply all the material things? Don't you know, darling, that I'd willingly give you everything I have and start from scratch again? Couldn't you possibly forget your damned independence for once?"

"Independence!" gasped Jessica, going slack in his

183

arms. "I don't care that about my independence while you're around!" and she snapped her fingers rather feebly. "Why I——"

"Say that again," he said and gave her one or two quick kisses.

"No, I won't," retorted Jessica, suddenly remembering Paula—and also that, in her saner moments, she prized her independence very highly.

"Listen, my darling." Ford turned her gently to face him. "You and I have been in great danger of losing the one thing that really matters. But fortunately you have an intelligent sister who believes in plain speaking, so we have a chance of retrieving it. Please tell me quite truthfully: why did you have this ridiculous idea that you didn't want to marry me, after all?"

"It—it wasn't that I didn't want to," Jessica whispered.

"What was it, then?" He dropped a kiss on the top of her bent head.

"I thought you—didn't want me—that you were only holding to the engagement because you'd made a quixotic gesture and wouldn't go back on it."

"But I've told you a hundred times," he exclaimed with impatient exaggeration, "that there was nothing quixotic about my proposal. If you want the crude and discreditable truth, I was determined to have you for my wife after that first evening, only——"

"Ford!"

"Of course I was," he reiterated rather angrily. "That was why I had to make sure that good-looking ass, Forrest, wasn't after you. But I knew it was no good hurrying you too much, and I deliberately thought out ways of coaxing or bribing you."

"Was *that* why you were willing to let me have the house on those ridiculous terms?"

"Of course. I told you—there was nothing quixotic about my behaviour. It was all rather disgraceful and calculated. And then, when you were ill and worried about the future of the twins, I knew I'd got a trump card and played it shamelessly."

"Ford, don't talk of yourself like that! Did—did you want me so much?"

He nodded.

"But why didn't you tell me so?"

"Because I was afraid you wouldn't take me then. I knew you weren't in love with me, and I thought my only chance was to put everything on a basis of mutual convenience. Besides"—he smiled a little grimly—"I suppose, in my heart, I was a bit ashamed of what I was doing and——"

"But, darling, there was nothing to be ashamed *about*. You've been an angel to me and the twins always. And if in return you hoped that I'd come to love you, what was wrong with that?"

His smile became less grim and, taking her face between his hands, he kissed her slowly again.

"I dare say one always feels a bit mean if one holds all the material advantages," he said.

"Only very generous, absurd people like you," she returned softly.

"Well, anyway, that was why I couldn't make any real protest last night. When you told me that Mary and Forrest were willing to give the twins a home, I felt I'd been deprived of a weapon I should never have used in any case."

She smiled and shook her head slightly. But his mention of last night's conversation brought the real cause of refusal back to her mind. Only, somehow, now it was quite easy to be frank about it.

"Ford, all this was quite incidental, you know," she said slowly. "The real trouble was that I thought you were still in love with Paula Dryden."

"Still? Good Lord, I never have been in love with her."

"Well, then, what were you doing embracing her in your garage yesterday evening?" cried Jessica with an unexpected little spurt of jealous anger. "And beside my car, too," she added, as though that made the offence worse.

"I was not embracing her." Ford was suddenly quite cool and positive.

"You were! I saw you!"

"You jealous little snooper!" he exclaimed with a delighted laugh, and caught her in his arms again.

"What you saw, my darling, was Paula embracing me. There's a good deal of difference, you know."

"But you had your arms round her."

"Had I?" He grinned reflectively, but without embarrassment. "Well, when a girl you've known as a school-kid hangs round your neck and cries, it's a bit difficult to remove her painlessly without taking hold of her."

"O-oh."

"Satisfied?" He looked more pleased and amused about her jealousy of Paula than she had ever seen him about anything else, and she was not quite sure whether she wanted to slap his cheek or embrace him.

"Were—weren't you ever in love with her?"

"Never," he stated categorically.

"It was just that she—was in love with you?"

"Oh, no. She's an emotional little idiot, who luxuriates in sentimental scenes between engagements," Ford stated rather brutally. "And, since we've known her since she and Angela were at school together, I naturally come in for the backwash sometimes."

"Well, you can't come in for it once we're married," Jessica objected quickly. At which he laughed so much that she did slap his cheek rather hard. And then, in immediate contrition, threw her arms round his neck and kissed him.

"Oh, Ford, I'm sorry! I love you so, and I thought I'd lost you to her. You mustn't laugh about it. Only I'm sorry I hit you. It was awful of me!"

"Darling," he said, "I'd willingly be knocked black and blue for the pleasure of hearing you say afterwards that you were sorry, and it was all because you loved me. But, my silly little love, I'm not laughing at you. I'm just laughing for sheer happiness, to know that you care enough to be jealous."

"Oh, Ford!" She gave a protesting little laugh, as she pressed against him. "It's so unintelligent to be jealous!"

"Well, you need never be so again. I'll tell you, here and now, at the risk of putting myself in your power for the rest of my life—there's never been, and there never will be, any woman but you, so far as I'm concerned. You knocked me straight into your hunting bag that evening you came and asked me to reduce the rent."

"Ford, what an *awful* way of putting it!" she protested, but she laughed and kissed him happily. "And to think Uncle Hector imagined he'd have done the job better himself," she murmured in contented parenthesis.

"Uncle Hector? Oh, he's not the really helpful relation," Ford declared scornfully. "There's only one member of your family calculated to put things right when you've got them muddled up, and that's Judy, bless her heart!"

"Oh, Judy!" With an affectionate little laugh, Jessica suddenly remembered her sister's determined, but blessed, interference. "She and Tom are probably dying to know what has happened. They must still be wondering, poor pets, if they're going to live at The Mead with Mary and David or at Oaklands with you and me."

"Well, we'll go and put that straight now," Ford announced with decision.

And, smiling and with their arms around each other, they went to find the twins.

OMNIBUS — The 3 in 1 HARLEQUIN
only $1.75 per volume

Here is a great new exciting idea from Harlequin.
THREE GREAT ROMANCES — complete and
unabridged — BY THE SAME AUTHOR — in one
deluxe paperback volume — for the unbelievably
low price of only $1.75 per volume.

We have chosen some of the finest works of four
world-famous authors . . .

SARA SEALE

JANE ARBOR

ANNE WEALE

ESSIE SUMMERS ②

. . . and reprinted them in the 3 in 1 Omnibus.
Almost 600 pages of pure entertainment for just
$1.75 each. A TRULY "JUMBO" READ!

These four Harlequin Omnibus volumes are now
available. The following pages list the exciting
novels by each author.

Climb aboard the Harlequin Omnibus now! The
coupon below is provided for your convenience in
ordering.

Sara Seale

Omnibus

Her natural talent for creating the very finest in romantic fiction has been acknowledged and enjoyed by a great many readers since very early in Miss Seale's career. Here, we have chosen three perfect examples of her best loved and most cherished stories.

. . . . CONTAINING:

QUEEN OF HEARTS . . . when Selina presented herself to her new employer at Barn Close, the exclusive country hotel in Coney Combe, Devonshire, Max Savant had one thought, to send this "child" on her way. Now, it was impossible for him to imagine himself, or his hotel being without her. But, he must, for he has just become engaged to Val Proctor . . . (#1324).

PENNY PLAIN . . . at Plovers Farm, near the village of Chode, in England, Miss Emma Clay is employed as assistant and companion to the rather spoilt young lady, Mariam Mills. Their relationship proves to be rather stormy, not the least cause of which is the country vet, in his country tweeds, the uncompromising Max Grainger . . . (#1197).

GREEN GIRL . . . Harriet listened to the incredible suggestion that she marry this total stranger and thus solve her dilemma, and the trouble which he himself was in. Whilst she knew full well that her own plight was quite hopeless, instinct warned her that Duff Lonnegan's trouble was far more serious than even he knew . . . (#1045).

$1.75 per volume

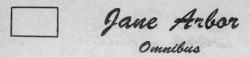

Jane Arbor
Omnibus

Jane Arbor chooses inspiring locations, peopled with the most life-like characters, — then inter weaves her gripping narratives. Her achievements have brought her world renown as a distinguished author of romantic fiction.

. . . . CONTAINING:

A GIRL NAMED SMITH . . . Mary Smith, a most uninspiring name, a mouselike personality and a decidedly unglamorous appearance. That was how Mary saw herself. If this description had fitted, it would have been a great pleasure to the scheming Leonie Crispin, and could have avoided a great deal of misunderstanding between Mary, Leonie and the handsomely attractive Clive Derwent . . . (#1000).

KINGFISHER TIDE . . . Rose Drake was about to realize her most cherished dream — to return to the small village of Maurinaire, France. To manage her aunt's boutique shop produced grand illusions for Rose, but from the very day of her arrival, they were turned to dismay. The man responsible was the town's chief landowner and seigneur, a tyrant — living back in the days of feudalism . . . (#950).

THE CYPRESS GARDEN . . . at the Villa Fontana in the Albano Hills in Italy, the young, pretty Alessandra Rhode is subjected to a cruel deception which creates enormous complications in her life. The two handsome brothers who participate come to pay dearly for their deceit — particularly, the one who falls in love . . . (#1336).

$1.75 per volume

Anne Weale

Omnibus

The magic which is produced from the pen of this famous writer is quite unique. Her style of narrative and the authenticity of her stories afford her readers unlimited pleasure in each of her very fine novels.

. . . . CONTAINING:

THE SEA WAIF . . . it couldn't be, could it? Sara Winchester the beautiful and talented singer stood motionless gazing at the painting in the gallery window. As she tried to focus through her tears, her thoughts went racing back to her six-teenth birthday, almost six years ago, and the first time she set eyes on the sleek black-hulled sloop "Sea Wolf", and its owner, Jonathon "Joe" Logan . . . (#1123).

THE FEAST OF SARA . . . as Joceline read and re-read the almost desperate letter just received from cousin Camilla in France, pleading with Joceline to come and be with her, she sensed that something was terribly wrong. Immediately, she prepares to leave for France, filled with mis-givings; afraid of learning the reason for her cousin's frantic plea . . . (#1007).

DOCTOR IN MALAYA . . . Andrea Fleming des-perately wanted to accompany the film crew on the expedition, but Doctor James Ferguson ada-mantly refused stating that if she went along, he would refuse to guide them. But, Guy Ramsey had other ideas, and cunningly devised a scheme whereby Andrea would join them — in a manner which the Doctor could not oppose . . . (#914).

$1.75 per volume